The Dead House

Praise for *The Things We Lose, The Things We Leave Behind*

'I know of no writer on either side of the Atlantic who is better at exploring the human spirit under assault than Billy O'Callaghan.' Robert Olen Butler, Pulitzer Prize winner

'O'Callaghan's protagonists may have a "predilection for melancholy" but nevertheless there are touches of hope in how they seek to take control of their lives, moments of action which serve as valuable counterpoints and contribute much to the texture of the volume …' *Irish Examiner*

'The elegant force of Billy O'Callaghan's prose is immediate and impossible to recover from. He is one of Ireland's finest short-story writers.' Simon Van Booy, Frank O'Connor Award winning author of *Love Begins in Winter*

'O'Callaghan's ability to use words to convey emotion is astonishing … The words coming up from the page and wrapping around you, transmitting that emotion, the aching from the core of the piece into the reader themselves … A delight to read, with strong, immediate prose, a distinctive style that becomes a thing of beauty.' *The Red Curtain*

BILLY O'CALLAGHAN was born in Cork in 1974 and is the author of three short-story collections: *In Exile* (2008), *In Too Deep* (2009) and *The Things We Lose, The Things We Leave Behind* (2013), the title story of which earned him the 2013 Bord Gáis Energy Irish Book Award for Short Story of the Year.

The recipient of literature bursaries from the Arts Council in 2010 and Cork County Council in 2015 among several other honours, including the Molly Keane Award and the George A. Birmingham Award, his work has been broadcast on RTÉ Radio 1's *Book On One*, *Sunday Miscellany* and the Francis MacManus Awards series. He has also been shortlisted on four occasions for the RTÉ/PJ O'Connor Award for Radio Drama. Over the past fifteen years, his stories have appeared in many literary magazines and journals around the world, including *Absinthe: New European Writing, Alfred Hitchcock Mystery Magazine, The Bellevue Literary Review, Bliza, Confrontation, The Fiddlehead, the Forge Magazine, Hayden's Ferry Review, the Kenyon Review, the Kyoto Journal, London Magazine, Los Angeles Review, Narrative Magazine, Southeast Review, Southword, Versal* and *Yuan Yang: A Journal of Hong Kong and International Writing.* This is his first novel.

The
Dead
House

... the past holds constant sway ...

BRANDON

First published 2017 by Brandon,
an imprint of The O'Brien Press Ltd,
12 Terenure Road East, Rathgar,
Dublin 6, D06 HD27, Ireland
Tel: +353 1 4923333; Fax: +353 1 4922777
Email: books@obrien.ie
Website: www.obrien.ie

ISBN: 978-1-84717-887-9

1 3 5 7 9 10 8 6 4 2
17 19 21 23 24 22 20 18

Printed and bound by CPI Group (UK) Ltd, Croydon, CR0 4YY.
The paper in this book is produced using pulp from managed forests.

Published in
DUBLIN
UNESCO
City of Literature

To Nellie and Peggy,
my grandmothers,

for the stories they gave me and give me still.
Sometimes, when the wind lifts
the dead still sing.

Acknowledgements

Books owe their lives to several people in a myriad of small but critical ways.

This story had been in my bones for years, decades, but it wasn't until Chang Ying-Tai and I set out to explore the Beara Peninsula, back in 2011, that I found the way of letting it be told. So, if it wasn't for her, there'd be no *The Dead House*. I owe her a lot, including that.

Others, too, mattered more than I can say. These are the ones who helped stoke the fire, or who kept me going with their belief when, on occasion, my confidence hit the dirt: Pete Duffy, Ronnie McGinn and Billy McCarthy, fellow scribes and my Rambling House-mates; and also Ann Riordan, Emma Turnbull, Denise and John Juliano, Cliodhna Lynch, Julia, Florian, Valentin, Helmut and Christine – the wonderful Schwaninger family, Sylvia Petter, Jack Power, Shoko Kanenari, Emilio José Bonome Ares, Yasemin Yazici, Seda Peksen and Aysu Erden. Deserving of my deepest and most sincere thanks are Martin McCarthy and Brian Whelan, friends and writers whose opinions I value more than those of anyone else, for reading and encouraging when no one else wanted to know.

It hardly needs saying, but I'll say it anyway, that my family are the reason I am anything at all. Martin, Kate and my great pal, Liam, who these days is the cause of nearly all my smiles; Irene, Yann and Jazz, who live my writing with me; and, of course, my parents, Liam and Regina, the most generous hearts I know, the ones who hold it all together and who keep us going when we stumble.

Beyond the writing, though – because, for me, the writing is usually the easy part; it's the living, to paraphrase the great Kris Kristofferson, that's hard – this book owes its existence to my agent and friend, Svetlana Pironko, of the Author Rights Agency, who fights my battles for me.

I must also acknowledge Cork County Council (and, in particular, the wonderfully supportive Library Arts Officer, Sinead Donnelly) for the

Literature Bursary in 2015, which let me spend precious time contemplating ways of getting a long-festering idea finally down on paper.

And finally, my gratitude to the staff of The O'Brien Press/Brandon Books, especially my patient, put-upon editor, Ide ní Laoghaire, for wrestling my words into such beautiful print; and, most of all, to Michael O'Brien, for seeing in my work what I always hope is there.

Walking

I walk ahead
– Just out of reach
Of the ocean's polished claw – a body
Observing the West Cork sun
Through rusted eye
– Hooked,
Hauled in,
And smashed,
And smashed again against the side.

A white and shivering skin
Assembles on the clawed floor.

I am afraid to turn and find
Only myself,
The sea,
And the wind.

Andrew Godsell (1971-2003)

Prologue

Tonight, I have a story to tell, one that for years I've kept buried, one that I'd hoped could have remained so forever. But the circumstances of the past several hours have brought everything once again to the surface, and I can no longer deny the things I've seen.

This is the truth as I know it to be, this is what I remember. At the very least, I want this to stand as a kind of confession. No, not only want. Need. Even now, I find myself clinging to the idea that some vital and previously overlooked detail will reveal itself, some glint sparking away in the dark distance with a final offer of salvation, something I have long misread or overlooked. God, hope, something. Clinging to logic in the face of every contradiction. Because time, as we all know, can blur things. But maybe it can also, in its way, bring clarity. I only hope that, with so much at stake, I have not waited too long to speak of this.

And if it should prove that I am deluding myself, that talking changes nothing, then tell me, please, if you can, what choice do I have? Hoping for the best, even in the face of certain worst, is how we all live our lives. Isn't it the reason why so many of us pray?

I suppose, in the final analysis, this story will hang on a single burning question:

Do you believe in ghosts?

Because that's really where it begins, with belief. We glimpse or experience something that defies explanation and we either accept the stretch in our reality or we choose to turn our heads away. It's a question that torments even philosophers: *Do you believe?* Our minds build our worlds for us, setting a line between what is acceptable as truth and what is not. We are conditioned to doubt the reality of the supernatural, and encouraged to assume that our world holds nothing more than the details of its surface. There is little about life as we have come to know it that can't be explained away on some basic scientific level. Yet when the wind howls, and we find ourselves alone with only the yellow pool of a guttering candle to hold back the darkness, our instinct, perhaps our innate need for something above and beyond, still screams otherwise.

That is, as I say, where it begins. With belief. I've seen, and the truth is that even now, with all that has happened and all that seems to be happening again, a part of me remains uncertain. The stains of scepticism are just as hard to scrub away as those of faith. What I do know is that, for me at least, the past simply will not remain the past. The dead refuse to rest, or even to lie still. And I am not asking you to believe. I ask only that you give yourself time and space to consider the question, and that you listen, with an open mind. Because this is something I need to tell.

Part 1

The Dead House

My name is Michael Simmons. I am married to Alison, and the father of one child, a daughter, Hannah, who is almost seven now, and our reason for bliss. Home for us is South-well, a small village on the Cornish coast. Our house, a mile and a half out, is a modest but ample stone-build that sits on its own wood-backed acre overlooking the sea. It is a place that holds the illusion of loneliness, yet lies within easy calling distance of the church bell. An ideal compro-mise. And we could not have chosen a more beautiful place to live than Southwell, positioned as it is among the folds of land and distinguished by steep streets and alleyways and lots of outlying greenery, the sort of place perfect for children. Even on the sodden days of winter, it retains a peculiar beauty. The air is clean, we can walk the cliffs, swim during the summer months or search for amber on the beaches. Cars drive slowly along its narrow roads, and everyone knows everyone else by name.

I am retired now, benched prematurely following a minor health scare, the mildest of heart attacks, and as a family we are comfortable without actually challenging the threshold of serious wealth. Fine Art has, for me, been a relatively lucra-tive business. I put in the hours, of course, the better part of twenty years' worth, initially with an agency and then, once I'd established my name and collected the requisite tally of contacts, in a freelance capacity. I represented a small but not inconsiderable stable of talent, painters mostly, but a few sculptors too, and even a practically famous Lithuanian conceptual artist. Still, I don't miss a thing about the paper chase, and the idle life seems most of the time crafted with me in mind, though I can, on occasion, be coaxed back to the table, when the money is right or a duty feels owed, to serve as a middleman of sorts, mainly providing a letter or phone call of introduction for one or another of my former clients directly to an artist who might still be within my reach.

Between our savings, pension and this occasional side income, we get by.

Alison and I met relatively late. I was nearing forty and had some three years on her, and we were at that point in our lives where the loneliness into which we'd settled had brought its own kind of unambitious contentment. I'd accepted, as a great many single people do once they hit middle age, that love, or anything even approaching the notion of love, had passed me by. Ali had been married once before, unsuccessfully. But that happens. And our coming together surprised us both. We could be happier, I suppose, but not much happier.

She's Irish, which adds a nice colour to our existence.

The Dead House

She was born in a small Wicklow village about twenty miles outside Dublin. It has since been absorbed by the city and is unrecognisable now from the place she'd known growing up, but twenty miles seemed to measure itself differently in those days, and her accent retains quaint elements of country, a lag or elongation that coats certain words. Sometimes she misses home, the nature of the place, the country as a whole, its pace, its softness, but there is comfort for her in knowing that we are always only a short flight away and we manage to get across two or three times a year, to take a cottage in Connemara or Clare, to sit in the pubs, explore the Burren, the islands. Alison wants Hannah to know her roots, and to feel at home there. Which is only right.

Though she and I first met in a romantic sense some nine years ago, we'd known one another a little longer than that. Existing on the outskirts of a shared business, we often had occasion to speak on the phone and kept up a relatively regular dialogue through email. We'd even been in the same room together, without actually colliding, on at least a couple of occasions, at some party or exhibition, and so we'd glimpsed one another from afar. What I'd seen then was a willowy, flowing woman looking half a decade younger than the facts, her raven hair tied up in a way that seemed to heighten her delicacy. Slight and pale-skinned, ethereal in certain falls of light. The sight of her made it hurt to breathe. She owned a small gallery in Dublin's Temple Bar, two floors of whitewashed space that exhibited more than its share of heavyweights and drew some decent footfall, and over the previous few years she'd hung and sold paintings by a number of my artists. I liked dealing with her because she was always straight when it came to money, a rare enough trait among art dealers, and because she showed a genuine appreciation, even passion, for the work she chose to display. More than that, though, I simply enjoyed chatting with her. We were always easy with one another, and with the benefit of hindsight the scent of something more between us seems apparent. But any blame for hesitation rests with me; I was the one who preserved the distance. I'd been through a couple of relationships, not serious exactly but of the kind that left marks, and I suppose I was afraid of making a fool of myself, and of ruining something potentially beautiful.

★

When you've made business your life, you get into a mindset where the world is concerned, and it can be difficult to let go. There is something safe and assuring about the ache to be at your desk, near a phone, a computer, to be able at a minute's notice to send out photographs of work, to negotiate, haggle, cajole from the chair you know and that knows you, all the while gazing out on the black-and-white-lit waters of the Thames and at the passers-by either half-clad in the sun or else wrapped and hunched against the rain. You are in control there, you know the environment, the cafés and restaurants, you have a routine set in granite and you know which boundaries to press and the point at which they'll snap.

Who has time for house-warming weekends?

'Come on, *Consiglieri*,' Maggie said, her voice filling the office from the speaker phone, full of mock threat. 'Make time.'

She was one of my artists and, more than that, one of my few truly close friends. Maggie Turner. I'd discovered her some years earlier, by the purest of accidents, and took all the credit I could from that, though she'd have been picked up sooner rather than later anyway because there is just no possible way in the art world that you can get by for any significant length of time being that good without somebody finally sitting up and taking notice. But I was the first, and that seemed to count for something.

The Dead House

I'd come to Manchester at the invitation of someone I had met at a party and didn't even remember but who'd happened to corner me at precisely the right moment of insobriety. Maggie's genius announced itself, admittedly as a suggestion yet, through a single, vicious watercolour being used as filler to bulk out an exhibition of graduate work from the local college of art and design. I'd been to a thousand of these events, but did my duty, moving around the room, trying to give every piece its chance, wishing with every step that I was somewhere else, anywhere else. Nodding when nodding seemed appropriate, pausing to consider technique, use of space, the authority of a brushstroke, perspective, shadow, and all the while conscious of the covert stares, the almost frenzied angst of twenty kids feeling themselves mere feet and then inches away from an actual future and already seeing the twinkle of the stars. I can't say precisely what I was hunting. A trace of the indefinable, I suppose. A suggestion of more. Something. You get a sense of it, if it's there. None of the work was particularly bad; these kids would all go on to make decent enough livings teaching GSCE Art or following the potentially lucrative graphic-design road into advertising, and maybe, on the side, just to fulfil a need or to nourish their enduring delusions, peddling a painting or two a year to clubs or societies or libraries, or to people who think it possible to buy their way into whatever currently passes for good taste. But all had the aura of sameness. Except hers.

She was still a year from finishing, and not even in attendance. They'd hung her painting, along with a few other junior pieces, ostensibly to demonstrate the consistent excellence of the college, but I knew from having seen this trick turned before that the true intent of the gesture was to emphasise and magnify the quality of the more polished work. Which I suppose says something about the subjective nature of art, and something else again about the judgement of those who are supposed to know better.

To the untrained eye, her watercolour was not flamboyant. An expressionist seascape on paper, small and only competently mounted, and seemingly unfinished. Jutting reefs in cadmium and jet, a ribbon of ochre beach with something like a horse and rider chasing the distance, and everything else ribs of water and sky. I loved the muddy confluence of colours, the wrong shades that somehow made up the sea, the ichorous waves, and I loved the simple, unaffected way in which she signed her name, Maggie, in rose madder, as if the letters themselves, like a jut of off-colour crabgrass or the remaining spindles of some mangled picket fence, not only belonged there but had something more than the obvious to contribute.

'Are you sure?' she asked, her voice flimsy as dust, her eyes hard and wide, after I'd twisted an address from a grudging instructor and without call or warning arrived by taxi at her door. Afraid to believe me. Not ready to, I knew. Sometimes the prospect of a future can be daunting. She stood there, wrapped in a child's dressing gown, cerise pink, and denims with the knees worn or torn out, leaning a hip against the counter while I sat perched on the edge of the apartment's only armchair and breathed the pungent stench of underlying linseed even through the pot of Irish stew fermenting behind her on the stove.

'You painted the light,' I told her, knowing what I meant but not quite getting there with words. But it really was that simple. 'You realised what mattered most in what you saw. That's an instinct. A rare one.'

I didn't encourage her to drop out of college. That was her choice. I did say that I believed there was little more the college could teach her. Colleges and universities have their place, and their worth, and when it comes to something as indefinable as art they can knock the edges off mediocrity and help make it presentable. But when the edges are what actually matter, such instruction can be fatal. She kept her head down while I talked, and her lack of reaction made me afraid of silence, so I kept on and on, praising her style, her composition, but mentioning the flaws, too, in a feeble effort to preserve some balance, and finally just saying anything I could think of, simply to keep a sound going in the room. How much Manchester had changed since I'd last been up here but how some things never change, like the rain. A full minute after I ran out of air, she seemed to regain consciousness. She glanced around, as if registering her living space for the first time. The one-roomed flat was shabby, but not a mess. A cursory attempt had been made at dressing the narrow cot bed, a few cups and plates lay cluttering the sink, left over from breakfast and, likely, the night before. Ancient paperbacks lined the single shelf in the alcove above the small television set, mostly westerns and Golden Age science-fiction novels, a combination that seemed odd only until I came to know her, and in the corner beyond the window a small chest of drawers stood littered with trinkets, little porcelain ornaments of cats, dogs and horses, and a narrow fluted glass vase that held a single probably stolen and already wilting daffodil. Her parents were dead and she had a sister in Canada, Rosemary, married to a dentist. When I got up to leave, she embraced me, and when she stepped back I saw that her cheeks were streaked in tears. She was young then — twenty, twenty-one — a brittle, almost elfin creature with a shining teak cap of hair, a long, deceptively pretty mouth and the largest eyes I'd ever seen, the deep pond green of carnival glass that was sometimes almost yellow and sometimes veered to darker shades.

That first month I sold three of her paintings, and I moved maybe six to eight each year after that for the better part of a decade, at decent prices too as her name became more and more established. She never cared about money, never queried a sale. Along the way, there were fallow periods when her work would change direction and we'd have to endure six or nine months of drought before she could again bring herself to produce anything saleable, and during those times I'd call on the phone or pay her frequent visits, not to try and press her into production but simply to chat, to touch base, take her out for coffee or lunch and, without discussion, to help her out with rent arrears, float her enough to get by. Her naivety kept her alive, I think, and I came to love her like a little sister.

The most recent dry period was different. A year, maybe a little longer. The span of time bothered me less than the nature of it. Inevitably, there'd been a man involved. Pete, a handsome city type, all briefcase and umbrella, something in an area of finance that to everyone but the law sounds

like a monumental con. They'd met through friends, at a
party, I think, and for a while she was all in, smitten by his
appetites and ambitions, even going so far as to start whispering words of marriage. I worried about her. Over the
years, there'd been men, one or two decent enough, the rest
not, but somehow she'd managed to remain an innocent,
if a scarred one. And an avowed romantic, the kind who
shatters when dropped. I wanted more than anything for
her to be happy and didn't give a damn, really, if she never
touched a brush again. But I knew from early on that she'd
made another wrong turn. It was clear to me, even without
having to see the bruises. When she spoke on the phone
the marks were in her voice, not a tremor exactly but a
shadow of something – pain, fear, whatever. An underlying
understanding of the dark. I'd met Pete only once. He was
tall and thin, not muscular but with a kind of threatening
hardness, and nurtured these long, still silences that made
you swallow and want to look away. Maggie would laugh
whenever I asked if she was all right, or at my offer, no
questions asked, of a bed for the night or for as long as she
needed, should she ever feel like bailing. Laugh as if I'd just
landed the punchline to the month's hottest gag, and say
no, thanks but no, she was fine, that it was nothing, just an
argument, the usual, that she'd been working too hard or

that he had. And then, some months on, I got a call from
Canada, from Rosemary, asking if I knew that Maggie had
been hospitalised. I didn't, which hurt more deeply than I
could have said. What I found waiting for me was carnage:
severe bruising to her throat, mouth and eyes, two cracked
ribs, a broken right wrist – mercifully not her painting
hand. The nurses had had to shave the hair on one side of
her head so that they could put a horseshoe of twenty-two
stitches into the scalp above her left ear. From where she'd
caught her head on the edge of the door, she explained,
unable to look at me, her voice birdlike with shame. When
I saw her in the bed, smashed into so many tiny pieces, I
wanted to cry, and within seconds began to wonder how
I'd go about getting hold of a gun. It never went further
than that, but there was a very real moment when I believe
I could actually have been capable of committing murder.

She had to get out, and she did. The law's interest in
what had occurred was sympathetic but fleeting, because
domestic-abuse cases are always complicated. A young
officer, a woman in clothes so plain she might as well have
carried a sign around her neck, came and sat at the bedside. You could tell by the set of her mouth and by her
eyes, which shifted in slow drags back and forth between
Maggie in the bed and where I stood leaning against the

window sill, that she'd been doing this twice a week for years and knew all the likely computations by heart. In a voice trained to the gentle, she told us that they'd investigate the matter to its fullest extent, and would try to make life as difficult as possible for the bastard. They'd show up at his workplace, make a big deal of requesting to search his desk, his car, confiscate his clothes so that they could scrutinise for traces of blood, hair and skin fibres. They'd even drop a few insinuations to his colleagues, particularly his female colleagues, so he'd know that everyone knew. But, she added, lowering her stare to the floor, it would be best not to expect too much, because the likelihood of pinning anything solid on him would be next to impossible. Despite a very real and explicit medical report, which was unequivocal in stating that the injuries Maggie sustained were one hundred percent consistent with a prolonged and particularly brutal assault, the evidence against the accused was circumstantial at best, and too heavily reliant on hearsay. He'd been careful, which suggested that he'd done this before, and the odds on achieving a conviction were thin to the point of anorexic. In fact, the case was unlikely even to make it as far as trial. Nevertheless, the officer was as good as her word, and Pete was harassed with three separate unannounced visits to his place of work, once even timed to coincide with his lunchtime absence from the office. Finally, when every avenue of inquiry had been exhausted, he was brought in for questioning and, as a way of inflicting as much discomfort as possible, held for the maximum allowable number of hours in a small, cold, windowless cell. Inevitably, on the advice of his solicitor and because he was intelligent and maybe experienced enough to understand the rules of play, he denied everything, and then a young woman came forward who was willing to swear under oath that he'd been with her on the night in question. The entire night. Her lie was obvious from half a mile away but the police were left with no option but to issue a release and grudgingly drop all charges.

Three weeks later, Maggie checked herself out of the hospital and into my care. At that time, I was leasing a two-bedroomed apartment in Kensington, a comfortable, spacious second-floor pad in Connaught Village, and I set her up in the spare room, with lots of good spring-time light and a south-facing view over Hyde Park. She spent most of those first days and weeks of recuperation stretched out on the sofa, swaddled in heavy sweaters or an old flannel nightgown, watching endless recycles of bargain hunting, property renovation and cookery programmes, and trying not to think about the world beyond my walls, trying to forget the person she'd so recently been. Sometimes, if I kept on enough and because my kitchen skills were barely a step evolved from abject, I was able to coax her into dressing and we'd eat out at one of the local restaurants. Such evenings were, for the most part, quite pleasant, but I could recognise the effort they required of her and the toll they took, and so mostly we fell for the recklessly unhealthy but far more convenient option and dined in on Chinese or Indian takeaways, food that could be ordered by number and eaten in a sprawl.

And then, one night, while watching the round-up of the day's football fixtures on the late news, she leaned across and kissed the corner of my mouth. 'I'm almost ready to leave,' she said, 'if that's okay with you. But I just wanted to say thanks.'

She looked better, though not yet quite right, and all I could think about was the warmth of her lips, what it had meant and what it might yet mean. I nodded, and pulled on a state of calm I didn't truly feel.

'What's the plan?'

'Ireland.'

She'd been there once before, she said, years ago, when she was just a girl, and I saw by the smile that, in her mind, she had already returned.

The Dead House

*

She spent that late March and early April in West Cork, alone, touring the Beara Peninsula in a hired car, stopping with each night's darkness at the first guest house that offered itself, spending as much of each day as possible outside, exposed to the rigours of the natural world, drinking in the scenery and sensations. The worst of her marks had faded, her hair had grown back and been cut into a presentable, if somewhat boyish, shape, one that passed for fashionable as long as you had no understanding of just how little style and fashion actually mattered in her world. But even though she was nowhere near fully healed, she had to go, had to do this. She ached, she said, for the solitude of the mountains and the sea. And I understood. Part of it was running away, because there are times when we all need escape, if only to assure ourselves that we still possess some modicum of that courage, and part had to do with searching for the things she'd lost and given up, the things that helped make her who she was. I think, after all she'd been through, she just needed to start feeling like a complete person again.

'This place is everything,' she said, on the phone. 'Even the air has wildness. I feel as if I'm out here collecting colours.' This was the third or fourth night, and she had just left Bantry and stopped off in Glengarriff, at a hotel called The Eccles, a quaint, old-fashioned place with great rates, decent food and breathtaking views out over the bay. She had already been for a walk, through the village and back and then down to where the ferry departed for the short jaunt across to Garnish Island. Seals clung like hulking black molluscs to the rocks and, out on the pier, a couple of elderly tourist anglers, German or Dutch, and brothers or at least relatives if the striking resemblance was genuine and not merely suggested by the matching knee-length shorts and green plastic windbreakers, stood talking-distance apart and, without ever disconnecting their gazes from the water, conversed in half-finished sentences during the lulls between casts. She'd have happily stayed for weeks, she told me, maybe even longer, because there was so much to see and feel around there, but she consoled herself with the thought that, since she was basically travelling in circles, the road would bring her back this way soon enough and she could still decide to stay then, if the yearning hadn't let up. Her plan, though, was to explore the peninsula in a slow anticlockwise sweep, keeping to a lazy fifteen or twenty miles a day limit, just a touch above walking pace, so that she could more thoroughly absorb the details of the landscape. Of course, the weather got in the way of everything good, the sky filthy shades of mud and rock, a west wind that opened you wide and got to know you from the inside out. But rain was this world's natural and permanent condition, a soft, relentless fur that muted distances and clung to the mountainsides like the smoke of fairy fires. To meet the place under better circumstances would mean to see only its lying face.

Something like a week passed then before I heard from her again, but the length of her silence didn't bother me. Fey to the point of self-absorbed, she'd always struggled with a comprehension of time and its implications. And busy with my own small world, I hadn't a chance to worry.

I'd just gotten in from a gallery opening in Chelsea where, as a favour to one of my contacts, I'd stood, pushed beyond my usual tolerance barrier to sift the three or four acceptable pieces of work from the clutter of greater dross, then forced myself to endure half a glass of foul red wine and spent an hour or so slipping in and out of airy conversations. When the phone rang I was in the kitchen, barefoot, buttering toast.

'I'm not coming back,' she announced, without as much as a word of greeting. 'Ever. I've seen a place and it's perfect. It's everything I want.'

I sat down with my tea and listened, knowing better than to interrupt. In gales of excitement, she described the small tied cottage in Allihies: a wild, beautiful, isolated ruin that dated to pre-Famine times, late eighteenth or early nineteenth century at least, with foundations that likely went back much further. Perched on its own hillside and spilling some five and a half acres down to the ocean and a rugged stretch of shoreline, it was blessed with the kind of scenery artists often spend entire lifetimes searching for and never finding. Going for less than the chorus of a song, too. A steal.

'You said a ruin.'

'Well, yes, I admit that the condition is a bit short of pristine, but what would you expect for nineteen thousand? In London, people probably spend that much on a garden shed.'

The truth, of course, lay between the lines. The cottage, which had never been wired or plumbed, was last occupied some time between the wars, and had stood empty and abandoned to the elements ever since. 'Short of pristine' was auctioneer-speak for the fact that it would require significant renovation both inside and out. The little remaining thatch had long since turned rotten and been overrun with rats, the chimney had fallen in, and there was clear evidence along the gable end of structural collapse, possibly at foundation level. A well, some fifty yards away towards the bottom of the first acre and now partially caved in, offered the only realistic access to drinking water.

But these were all problems that money could fix, and, as far as she was concerned, the true worth of this place went far beyond mere stone and mortar. She'd seen it from the road, in passing, just as the noon light seeped momentarily chalky through the bluish knuckles of rain-cloud, and the ocean beyond the fall of land stretched off into the distance as a shifting slate pocked with the dapple of an entire submerged galaxy. And that single fleeting glimpse had been enough to capsize her world.

'I can hardly put into words how this place makes me feel, Mike. There's such a sense of isolation here, like nothing I've ever known before. Out here, it really does seem as if you're cut off from the rest of existence. And I mean that in the best way possible. Because it's actually not that isolated at all. Not really. Allihies is only a few minutes by car and maybe fifteen or twenty on foot. It's a small village, but there's a decent-sized shop, a post office, a choice of pubs. More than enough to get by. And for bigger needs, there's always Castletownbere, the nearest town of any real consequence, probably not much more than half an hour back along the southern side of the peninsula. But, I don't know, it's like there are two kinds of reality out here. There are the facts, and then there's something else. Within about a minute of seeing the place, you get the sense that when a storm blows even the least gale, the walls very quickly close in. This might be the twenty-first century, but civilisation around here feels only barely removed from myth.'

The road out from Reentrisk to the cottage was narrow and full of twists, she said, a sort of boreen built with horses and, at a push, carts, in mind, and with a surface not always guaranteed to hold the weight of a vehicle. When the house first came into view below and on the right it was necessary to park the car on a verge and cover the last couple of hundred yards on foot, keeping to a suggestion of dirt pathway flanked and in places smothered with wild briar, down the steep hillside.

No artist could begin to hope for more than what she'd found: spectacular views of beaten hills and ocean, huge skies and, best of all, the light, a strange spectral light, peculiarly heavy and in a constant state of flux. Just breathing this air made you want to cry and laugh at the same time. Here the world had simplified itself down to rocks, ocean, sky, wind and rain; these because everything else was fleeting, and you felt overwhelmed by such a sense of permanence all around, by the realisation that what you could see in any one moment and in any direction had always existed and always would. Holy men built monasteries in places like this, trying to capture part of the alchemy that coaxed time into standing still. The immensity of so much wildness brought on a kind of melancholy, it dwarfed you, made you feel small beneath greater things, but it also made you feel oddly and fully alive. In the midst of such scale, she said, her awareness couldn't help but shift and become heightened.

Conditions inside the cottage were bad, apparently. Crumbling plaster, smashed windows, the stench of things dead and rotten, gulls, vermin and, in one of the two small bedrooms, the one that looked westward out onto the ocean, the whitened remnants of something bigger, a dog or fox, but now just a kindling of bones splayed in the natural order of its undisturbed collapse. The work involved in returning this place to some habitable state would, of course, be immense and daunting, but Maggie could see beyond all the problems.

Within an hour of her first sighting she had spoken on the phone with an estate agent in Castletownbere, a woman named Mairéad, who checked the company's books and came back almost immediately with the good news that her agency had it listed as an executor sale for a firm of Cork solicitors. The deeds were missing, lost if they'd ever even existed, but this was a minor legal issue common enough with such old properties, especially in rural areas, and could be easily overcome. They met the following morning and walked the site together. Mairéad was a short, smiling woman of about forty, with long reddish blonde hair and the sort of blushed complexion that seemed to suggest early onset menopause but may just have been the result of a morning spent chasing the clock and picking up the pieces in the aftermath of a hectic night. Armed with a small red plastic folder of printed information and a couple of Ordnance Survey maps, she led the way, pointing out the boundaries of the accompanying land and talking almost incessantly about the weather and what the area was like in summer, and about growing up on the other side of Allihies, how things had changed over the past few years and, more importantly, how much remained the same. She also provided Maggie with a list of reliable contractors who could see to the necessary refurbishments at a competitive price, but warned that the final tally was still likely to top out at a fairly high number, given the need for such a complete overhaul.

'Are you sure this is what you want?' she asked, considering Maggie after they had been through the carcass of the house and emerged again into the soft rain. Behind them, nests of young rats, disturbed by so much talk after being allowed to get by for so long without, screamed and chased frantic circles in the remaining thatch. 'This place has been empty a long time. Too long to be natural, really. And people talk. It's lonely out here, the kind of place where it'd be too easy to glimpse things. We have other properties, in much better condition, and with views that are just as stunning as this. They'd offer better value, too. A bit more up front but far less in the way of renovations. If you come back to the office we can go through them together. You won't be disappointed, I promise. We have some real beauties on our books at the moment. I'm sure we'll find something that you can move into immediately, if that's what you want.'

It was not her job to dissuade an eager buyer, but per-haps she was reacting to some felt vibration or had already absorbed hints of the place's past through the stories and rumours that tend to linger like mud stains in the col-lective consciousness of towns and villages everywhere. Most likely, though, she probably just wanted to do the right thing. Maggie's obvious fragility was hard to miss and impossible to ignore: eyes used to seeing beyond edges now fixated into a permanent, lost-looking stare, the brackets dimpling both ends of a mouth held slatted for too long, the vague sheen lingering after a period of swelling and discolouration in the softer pockets of skin.

But Maggie just smiled and shook her head, no. This place spoke to her, she said. She had no interest in looking at other houses, not now that she'd seen this, walked its ground, breathed its air. This, she said, with a smile that must have beamed from the greatest depths, was where she belonged.

And it was. I could feel it, too, even through the phone. I'd known it before, in other aspects of other lives. Such a level of passion can't be faked.

'I hate to ask,' she said to me, into a silence that had opened up between us, 'but I need money.'

She'd not produced a saleable painting in nearly a year, and after laying out cash on the place, which she'd eventually been able to negotiate down to the bedrock number of nineteen grand from the initial asking price of twenty-two five, had all but emptied her pockets. I finished my toast and told her between bites that it was no problem, that I'd have it in her account within a day or two. Which, looking back, is why I feel so responsible for everything that happened. Even if the place really was her perfect fit, I still sensed in my heart that she was making a terrible mistake.

In her state, such isolation would be anything but good for her. And yet, I said nothing. I enabled her, I suppose. I fed her habit and made it all too easy, too comfortable. But what else could I do? We were friends, closer than that, even. And she'd already been through so much. I wanted to help. I wanted her to be happy.

'Do you have any idea of a figure?'

I could feel her shrug.

'It'll be quite a bit,' she said. 'Mairéad has already spoken to an architect. And I want work to begin immediately. The most pressing issues need attending first, the structural problems, a new roof, plumbing, electrics. Just to get the place habitable.'

'What are we talking about? Roughly?'

'With what's left in my savings,' she said, and I could hear the tremble in her breath, 'I'll need another thirty thousand. But it'll likely run to higher. Can you manage that much?'

I didn't hesitate. I said I could.

★

A cursory survey clarified the magnitude of the property's many ills. The walls needed to be strengthened and secured, the foundations damp-proofed, the roof stripped away and new beams and thatch laid, new windows installed, new doors, a kitchen and bathroom, units and utilities, the well cleared and re-bored and an entire plumbing and heating system put in, along with a generator to supply power. From day to day, the scale of the project seemed overwhelming, yet within six weeks the major renovations were completed, and though the final costs far exceeded the original estimate, coming within whispering distance of the fifty-thousand mark, Maggie had only praise for the dedication of the contractors and the standard of their craftsmanship. She'd moved in towards the end of the second week, once the smaller of the two bedrooms had been made safe, slept on a roll-up mattress spread out across timber pallets, and mainly so as not to get in the way of the work spent the lengthening days of late spring either down on the beach or exploring the surrounding area, walking the hills and roads, chatting with locals, seeking out places of interest – the copper mines, the druids' circle, the cliffs and shoreline reefs where the cormorants nested, the ancient stone associated with the Children of Lir, one of the three great sorrows of Irish myth. Trying desperately to understand something of this place, she said, and to come to terms with its elemental wildness.

The Dead House

Because I'd promised, or at least grudgingly agreed, I flew into Cork early on the first Friday morning in June, hired a car at the airport and made the long drive west. Taking my time, allowing myself to enjoy the scenery and doing my best, though it went against every natural instinct, not to worry. The morning was warm and bright, as perfect as early summer ever gets, the sky that pale mottled blue of a robin's eggs, the fields everywhere lush with the growth of a good spring. I stopped off in Skibbereen, judging it a reasonable midway point, ate a massive fried breakfast in a cramped but lovely six-table café that kept the coffee coming as fast as I could get it down, and by eleven I was back behind the wheel. The radio was tuned to a station busily giving away tickets for an upcoming Van Morrison concert and playing a number of his songs, including some old gems that I hadn't heard in years but which took much of the hardship from the remaining two hours or so of road.

Quite what I'd been expecting is difficult to express, but the cottage looked magnificent in its setting. I pulled up behind three cars that were already lining the road's verge, killed the engine and got out to survey the view. In the sunshine, it truly was something to see, the sidling hills and verdant fields, the low, loose-stone boundary walls, the ditches overgrown with bramble and gorse, and beyond, a stretch of ocean silvery and bluish to a clear horizon. Allihies was still a couple of miles further on along the road, but no sound carried apart from the occasional screech of a passing petrel or gannet. We tend to smother our lives, collecting all the burdens we can carry, forever sweating the inconsequential. I drew and spent a deep whispering breath and, for the first time in several weeks, since Maggie's hospitalisation at least, felt my shoulders open up and the natural constriction in my chest give a little, and then a little more, and I began to understand.

Before I reached the bottom of the incline, the front door of the cottage opened and Maggie came outside at a little half-run. I stopped and set myself for the impact, but the feel of her against me was still beyond prediction. She wrapped me in a tight embrace and began to peck my face and mouth with tiny laughing kisses, and the only option was surrender. The transformation in her astonished me. Her hair had grown, thickening again to an alluring feminine fullness from the unfortunate severity of its recent crew-cut, she was barefoot and dressed in faded jeans and a sleeveless white cotton blouse, and it was as if the past had fallen away for her and she'd been reborn to a new level of freedom. Her smile simmered with love and happiness, and I held onto her and returned her kisses with all my strength, feeling a share of that newly found joy myself.

Then she released me and turned so that we could consider the scene together.

'Well? What do you think?'

'I suppose I've seen worse.'

She laughed and punched my arm. 'Asshole. Come on, let's get inside. You're the last to arrive. I wasn't even sure you'd actually come.'

I gave her my hand and let myself be led down the last few steps of the pathway. Then, just as we were about to enter the cottage, she stopped, put her arms around me and kissed me again. 'Thank you, Mike,' she sighed, and I could feel tears of relief in the soft press of her voice against my chin and throat. 'For everything. I'd have no one if I didn't have you.'

'You say that, and yet I've been here five minutes and you still haven't offered me a beer.'

'Beer. You've got a one-track mind, you know that? But come on. The others are already here. And there's someone I want you to meet.'

'Who?'

'You'll see.'

'Stop it.'

'Stop what?'

'What. That look. The smile.'

'I can't smile now? It's some kind of a crime to smile?'

'I'm warning you, Maggie. No games.'

But she had my hand again and dragged me inside, and I had no choice, now that I'd come this far, but to follow.

The cottage looked good. It looked and felt like a home. She'd spent the weeks well and had made great progress. There was still work to be done, with elements of the rawness that defined unfinished construction, but she'd clearly settled in and had already begun to put her mark on the place. The living room in particular was decked out in a very comfortable style, with the walls bare yet of art but painted soft shades of fandango pink and a yellow that she announced as babouche, and on the floor, at angles of their own accord, two large cheap rugs, one paisley, the other a seemingly random patchwork of greens and blues, helping to mask the chill of raw flagstone. I glanced around and saw, with some pleasure, that her books, the paperback westerns and science-fiction novels, Louis L'Amour, Zane Grey, Bradbury, Heinlein, had made the transition, too. They'd increased to a small horde over the preceding decade, and packed in upright back-to-belly fashion the three built-in shelves of the alcove beside the small, open fireplace.

Unquestionably, though, the room's best feature was the pair of tall, west-facing sash windows. Period pieces, or impressive reproductions, they dominated the space, presenting a most dramatic vantage out over the back acres to the shoreline and the ocean beyond. Already flooding the room with natural light, their promise of a red end to a long day seemed the perfect succour to an artistic heart.

Two women had been leaning towards one another in laughing conversation from either end of a cream faux-leather three-seater sofa but lapsed into silence as soon as I entered the room. The shape of their laughter lingered and for a moment they continued to hold their tilting pose, and my heart began to beat very hard when I recognised the woman nearest to me as Alison. A small hi-fi system in the corner facing the door filled the background with a series of unobtrusive fiddled airs and I could feel the jig-time insinuation churning through me like a second pulse.

Alison rose, and after a beat, the other woman did, too. Then Maggie appeared beside me with the can of promised beer, and the atmosphere seemed to shift and lose its heft. She made the introductions in a casual way, and I shook hands with the second woman first, a poet named Liz who had been a friend of Maggie's in London but who'd moved to West Cork a couple of years back. Her accent was all Galway but, preferring, as she put it, the reality of the south-west, she'd settled in Bantry now, which made them practically neighbours. She was young and pretty in that rough-hewn and slightly tarnished manner of those who only properly come to life on more esoteric plains. Late twenties, maybe thirty at a push, with a profusion of high and wildly piled straw-coloured hair, the sort of tight mouth well used to silence and about five inches worth of metal and plastic bangles weighing down her left wrist. A poet with two books published by a small press and a third scheduled to appear by year's end, she kept herself fed and found by teaching evening classes two nights a week in Bantry and running a Saturday workshop in Skibbereen, and also by reviewing books on a more or less weekly basis for two newspapers, one national, the other local.

'And I believe you already know Alison,' Maggie said, and Alison looked at her and nodded. Not knowing what else to do, I offered my hand and mumbled how pleased I was that after all the conversations and emails we were finally getting the chance to meet. 'Come on, people,' said Maggie. 'This is a house-warming, not a summit. What are we? Politicians? Enough with the handshakes. Make this a proper hello.'

Alison hesitated, then some barrier came down and her

laughter was back, and we embraced, kissing cheeks, like the friends we almost were and like the lovers we were soon to be.

Beside us, Maggie cracked open my can of beer and sucked up the sudden spout of froth. 'That's better,' she said, between sips. 'Now let the festivities officially begin.'

★

Once the initial awkwardness of our situation passed, the weekend took off in a happy, if more than slightly tipsy, direction. I have always been comfortable in the company of women, particularly beautiful women, perhaps because, from an early age, my expectations were curtailed by a strong awareness of my own limits. And, for the most part, women appeared to enjoy my company. Even now I'm not bad-looking, without in any way threatening the realms of handsome, but by my mid to late thirties I'd settled somewhere between twenty and thirty pounds over my ideal weight. I favoured the philosophical slant and chose to think of it less as having let myself go than as the simple, natural realignment of the inevitable, maybe even the genuine expression of my true middle-aged self. Because I am reasonably tall, and broad across the shoulders, the excess girth never hung too badly, not the way it can and does on some, but the extra weight softened me, made me less assured, or at least less significant, than I might once have been. Certainly less ambitious. And women sensed this, I think. Around me, they could relax and even risk a little flirting without having to worry that it would lead them in wrong directions. I'd enjoyed success in my chosen line of work and, as I've already mentioned, achieved a modest definition of financial security, but my talent, such as it was, lay largely in recognising the gifts that others possessed, and could be difficult in itself to quantify. So my achievements posed no threat to the greater balance. I dazzled no one, and when it came to thoughts of romance, women could look in my direction and just as quickly look away. And I learned to adapt, and as the saying goes, to accept the things I could not change. There is a point in life when a man gets used to being alone, and anything above and beyond that is a bonus.

We spent the Friday just chatting and catching up, revealing piece by piece the small truths of who we were. Maggie lay stretched out on her side on a large beige bean-bag on the floor, directing us towards one another, leading the conversations with questions to which she already knew the answers. The beer, and later on, the whiskey, made it easy to talk. And I felt happy and at home. We all did, I think. I enjoyed listening to Liz expound on some of the more remarkable aspects of this area and its history, particularly its ancient history, that misty corner of the past where myth and reality collude, and her passions seemed to mirror Maggie's own, as if they were each somehow fuelled by the same fire. Alison – being, like me, in the business side of the arts – displayed less of that intensity, less wildness, I suppose, but she looked relaxed, laughed readily and was clearly glad to be here. Somewhere in late afternoon, just before we attempted the chaos of a communal spaghetti Bolognese, she kicked off her shoes and tucked her feet up beside and beneath her on her side of the sofa. She'd painted her toenails a crimson that in the shaded living room deepened to the heavy maroon of newly drawn blood, and I tried not to stare but couldn't help myself. She knew, I think, and caught my eye several times. But she said nothing and didn't seem to mind. Looking back, it was probably all part of the flirtation ritual, though to me it felt like more than that. Maybe it was the whiskey or maybe something chemically fused, the sparks they sing about in songs, but I felt as if I could see inside her, as if through the tiniest of exposures she was revealing some part of herself that people usually never got to see.

The Dead House

We didn't turn in until well after midnight. Maggie and Liz shared a room, and a double bed, Alison scored a folding cot in the small second bedroom, and I was left with a blanket and the sofa. I lay awake for a long time, but when I did drift off, somewhere between two and three, I slept well, thanks in large part to the quantity of alcohol I'd consumed. Even so, I woke early, before seven. I boiled water for tea and drank it from a large mug while gazing out at the ocean. The day had opened pale and bright, with the promise of great things to come, and the flat chrome blanket of water kept an illusion of stillness that came apart only where it met the stabbing black shale flashes of the headland reef. After a few minutes, I felt the presence of someone else and turned to find Alison in the doorway, watching me. She couldn't sleep either, she said, taking the offered tea and helping herself to three spoonfuls of sugar. We sat at the small kitchen table then, neither one of us saying much. And it was nice, it felt right. I snatched glances at her and tried to absorb all the details without seeming to do so, and I know now, looking back on it all, that those were the minutes when I finally and truly fell in love.

Ragged still with sleep, she had on a pale blue cotton summer dress decorated with badly rendered clusters of green and yellow flowers, daffodils, I think, and a lemon-yellow wool cardigan draped over her narrow shoulders to protect against dawn's leftover chill. She kept her dark eyes low and half-lidded, raising them only occasionally to me and then smiling sweetly and with embarrassment, as if she'd been caught in the middle of something private.

'Let's go for a walk,' I said.

'Now?'

I shrugged. 'Just down to the water, see what all the fuss is about. At the very least, the air will do us good, help clear our heads. Maybe we'll even get lucky and find our appetites down there.'

We walked slowly, side by side, in silence. The grass, damp from the night's dew, was thick behind the cottage, and long and wispy as we moved down through the last acre and the ground became more uneven. With every step I was conscious of the eighteen inches or two feet of distance between us, and then, just as the narrow, broken path down onto the rocky beach revealed itself, I felt her hand slip into mine. Her skin was cool, and her grip had the loose delicacy of a child's. I tried to keep perspective, and told myself that she was wearing low heels and had only grabbed onto me for support against the uncertain footing, a fact that was more or less borne out by the way she drew back her hand as soon as the ground once more levelled out. But her retreat still left me fighting a sudden void. We came down onto the beach and stood a while, close enough that I could feel the soft, relentless pull and fall of her breathing, and the waves spilt hissing up towards us and broke clear except for their greyish fringes across the fine crushed sand. Though the air hardly moved, Alison drew her cardigan across her chest and held it closed in one fist just beneath her throat.

'It's beautiful here, but kind of lonely.' She glanced at me. 'Don't you think?'

I said I did.

'I could be happy in a place like this, but I'd need to have someone to share it with me. Imagine coming down onto this beach in the dead of winter, some dark morning in November with a gale blowing and these waves swollen waist-high, lashing the shore. I don't think I could stand to be here for that. Not on my own.'

'Maggie has had enough of people,' I said. 'She thinks she needs the isolation. I don't happen to agree with her, but I understand why she wants to get away. Her plan is to paint here, to get some real work done, and at least on her own she can't get hurt. She's been hurt enough already.' But I looked around and knew exactly what Alison meant, because I could feel it, too. The summer morning was a disguise, a delusion.

For now, though, it was pleasant to walk. And I was more content than I'd thought possible, simply getting to share this time with a woman like Alison. I tried not to dwell on it, or make more of it than it likely was, but I gave myself permission to enjoy these minutes, knowing well just how fleeting the state of happiness can be. We chose to follow the shoreline south-westward, because the cliffs rose in that direction and the outcroppings of rock ensured we couldn't go very far. That morning, I think, there was an unspoken need for boundaries. And with the ceaseless press of the ocean on our right I had a sense of having arrived at the edge of the world. There were no sounds beyond the gentle rushing of the waves and the steady crunch of our steps, and I only talked because Ali asked me questions, mainly to do with business, about work I'd recently sold and new work not yet finished but which already had me excited and might, if the price could be right, perhaps excite her, too. And then it was her turn, and she talked, of her own accord, about the pros and cons of living in Dublin, the theatres, the traffic, the increase in gang crime, the inner city's struggle to retain some tradition against the yuppified posturing and hard currency brag of the recent economic upturn, and the anomalous markets and old pubs that still abounded with Joycean characters, mock Georgian in everything but the loud swagger of their accents. She mentioned, too, without meeting my eye, that she'd been married, briefly, a hundred years ago, one of those eight-month mistakes that twenty-year-old girls sometimes make. A juvenile politico named Laurence, who talked endlessly of saving the world but who, it soon turned out, modelled the term 'selfish bastard' at professional catwalk level. Ready at a moment's notice wherever a placard could get him seen, anti-everything except spending other people's money, fawning over anyone who might conceivably buy him drink and crawling into bed with anyone in panties. Her mother had warned her, of course, everyone had, but at that age she could hear nothing beyond the singing of the birds. And then, one morning, after she'd just hung up on the umpteenth of his sluts, the clouds parted. When he woke, maybe an hour later, she had all of his belongings bagged and packed. Her stepfather stepped in, dealt with the paperwork and with a little money and a lot of menace made it all official, and she hadn't seen Laurence in something like twelve years and never wanted to see him again. The last she heard, he'd washed up in America, probably found himself some masochist with cash to burn who'd happily tolerate his brand of honeydew horseshit.

Ahead of us, the low cliffs pressed in and the beach narrowed and was eventually cut off by outcroppings of staggered reef. I caught movement and raised a hand to shield my eyes from the glare, but for the next few seconds the world was still.

'There's someone there,' I said, uncertain why the words troubled me. My voice was calm but unsteady. I cleared my throat.

'What?'

'Up ahead. On the rocks. A woman, I think. A girl.'

We stopped and stared. The reefs were dark layers in the near distance.

'What did you see?'

'I'm not sure. Movement. A girl, I think. With long dark hair, wearing something white. One of those glimpses that you catch when you're not really looking.'

She stared, and so did I.

'I don't see anything now.'

'No.'

'Could it have been a gull? Or the spray of a wave? I know it's calm but the water can really kick up when it hits a reef.'

'It looked like a person. A girl. She was just standing on the rocks, watching the distance. Just for half a second.

There and then gone.'

Alison considered the reefs a moment longer, then shrugged. 'Probably one of the locals, out gathering periwinkles. We used to collect them ourselves, when we were kids. My sister Helen and I. My father would take us out to Wexford for a couple of weeks every summer. We had relatives in a village along the northern Hook, just outside of a place called Fethard-on-Sea. Two of my father's sisters and an old woman who was either an aunt or a great-aunt of his. There was a pub called Conan's in the village that would take all the cockles and periwinkles they could get. The owner's wife used to pot them. At that age, I had no taste for them, though I wouldn't hesitate now, but I remember that the tourists couldn't get enough and would eat them straight from jars, set in clarified butter. Good for the soul, everyone said, though probably not the heart.' She slipped an arm inside the crook of my elbow. 'Come on, Mike. Let's go back. I think I could go some breakfast now.'

When we returned to the cottage, the others were up. Liz, cradling a huge cream and red polka-dot mug of steaming black coffee, sat at the kitchen table with her knees drawn up beneath her chin and her eyes limited to reluctant slits. Maggie stood at the stove, frying bacon and sausages, barefoot and bare-legged in just an oversized grey

T-shirt and a pair of pink, childishly modest panties that revealed themselves to the eye whenever she had need to reach for something. Her smile for us as we entered was full of insinuation, and we let it go without the least acknowledgement because there was nothing to be said. I sat down across from Liz, and Alison poured us both coffee from the pot and then took the seat beside me. The door had been propped open to my left to let in the air of the morning and in case anyone wanted to smoke, and from my place I could see down along the path we'd just taken, and the strip of shore dull in the distance against the shining water. But the reefs lay out of view. I told myself that what I'd glimpsed was nothing, my imagination stoked by a trick of the light, yet it bothered me.

'How was the beach?' Liz asked, addressing neither one of us in particular.

Alison smiled. 'Lovely. A bit cool down by the water at this hour, but lovely for a walk.'

'It's a beautiful morning,' I said, then seemed to cut myself off.

Alison glanced at me. 'Mike thought he saw something on the rocks.'

'Not something. Someone. A girl, I think. Have you noticed anyone around here the last few weeks, Maggie?'

She turned from the stove, thought about it, then shrugged. 'I don't think so. The workmen, of course. I probably just didn't take any notice. But there are houses around, and it's an easy walk to the village. No one owns the beach so I suppose there'll always be people passing by. You probably saw one of the neighbours. I've not really met anyone yet, except to say hello to a few in the village. But curiosity is part of the fabric of rural areas, isn't it? Especially with kids. Someone new moves in, they want to see. Now, who's having eggs, and how many?'

★

The day was a good one. Following a lazy breakfast, we queued for a turn in the shower, then piled into one car and set off to explore the peninsula. Maggie insisted on driving, and because Alison and I had the back seat to ourselves, and even though we sat quite properly apart from one another, the rear-view mirror was almost constantly active. I found it difficult to ignore such scrutiny without smiling or being annoyed, but Ali didn't even seem to notice. And, really, the landscape demanded the bulk of our attention. All around, the ground flowed in tumultuous order, a cascade of the wildest washed-out greens torn and split by jutting flashes of slate and limestone, hills and valleys away from the coastline, mountainsides sheer and striped in gorse, looking naked and somehow foreign, denied their usual pretence of softness by the clear and cloudless late morning. And always, everywhere, sealing in the picture, ocean. The shower had revived Liz, or at least succeeded in blunting the sharpest edges of her hangover, and she sat half-turned in the passenger seat and kept us entertained with a constant supply of talk, a passionate deluge of fairy tales and famine stories. Then, producing from her rucksack a badly browned and dog-eared paperback, she began to read for us some of the old poems attached to the blood and stone of this area, prayers and laments for men gone to sea or loved ones to America, presenting them first in their translated state and then, even though she was far from fluent but just so that we could hear the proper music of their rhymes and feel something of their aching melancholy, in the original Irish. And almost as an aside, she began to talk of the ancients. History haunted the present in places like this, she said, places that existed at a hard remove from the rest of the world, and the incessant closeness of so much storied past tended at times to skew the definition of reality.

Her poetry had always strived for some of that mythological and elemental flavour, but since returning to Ireland, and particularly since settling here in West Cork, she'd immersed herself in the ancient texts with intent towards writing an epic poem based on a piece of local lore. For thousands of years, she explained, dating from the earliest settlements and on through into the seventeenth century, Ireland had existed as a clan society obedient to a system of Brehon Law. High kings ruled from Tara, the royal seat in County Meath, but their control was rarely better than tenuous and the general consensus now accepted that the true power in each region almost certainly lay with the clan heads, the local chieftains. Liz had written long poems before, but nothing on such a grand scale, and, two years in, it still felt as if she'd barely broken the skin of the thing. But that didn't matter. Having finally released herself from thoughts of ever finishing, she was now, artistically speaking, exactly where she wanted to be: content within the beat of the work and learning, step by stumbling step, to walk on air.

'When studying the Irish, particularly the ancient Irish, it's important to understand that the only absolutes are the ocean and the sky. And when the rains come, even those definitions are lost. History here is a stew of fact and fable. Each is inseparable from the other, and trying to sift them apart is like trying to remove butter from toast. To get any feeling for it at all, you have to cede a place to magic.'

Beyond my window, the water glistened in a way that held and hurt my eyes, and I tried to imagine, as I often did in moments like these, what an artist might look for in such a scene, what details or precisions they'd catch that I would normally miss. Everything about the world ahead of me was colour – subtle shades shared out among the tumbling fields and flashes of shoreline, the rocks, waves and sky – and that, I knew, was a glimpse of magic, too, and an acknowledgement of my own failings. Because the water was blue, but not blue, it was grey, or green or a kind of burnt silver that seemed far beyond the scope of something as simplified as paint. It was all of those, and none of them, and only the right sort of eye could see, and recognise, and understand. As usual, I was seeing it as I tended to see everything: in too simplified a way. As usual, I was blind to the depths and stories of the world.

At Maggie's suggestion, we stopped, a little after noon, in Castletownbere, a small, bustling town with a busy harbour, and a beautiful place to be in the sunshine. Glad to escape the confines of the car, we strolled through the streets, stopping often so that the women could browse in the tourist shops, handle the roughly carved blackthorn walking sticks, select postcards from the racks and take turns trying on the flat tweed caps that filled them with delight and simply demanded to be bought.

From there, we lunched on toasted sandwiches and Beamish in one of the pubs at the top of the main street, Houlihan's, a purposely dark, cool place trying hard to act ten times its age, the exposed beams, bare stone walls and sawdust on the floor seeming so much the very definition of traditional that it was difficult not to entertain just the slightest scepticism. Still, the food was good and the stout even better. I had a pint and then a second, Alison and Liz showed restraint with glasses, and Maggie, our driver, had to tolerate an orange juice and made no effort to hide her disappointment. Across the room, an extremely old man and what looked to be his grandson or even his great-grandson, a boy of no more than about ten, played solemn, stumbling reels on fiddles burnished by firelight, oblivious to everyone and everything except one another and the music.

When we left the pub, a little after two o'clock, the day had deepened. The air seemed golden, and calm. We walked back to the harbour, close to where we'd parked, and idled for a while watching the cars in a long, pent-up line take turns at reversing, with considerable difficulty, down a steep

ramp and onto the deck of a small ferry. Tourists from one
of the several parked coaches milled about in packs, mostly
middle-aged or elderly, American by their accents and
ambitiously dressed in knee-length shorts and sandals, but
some kids too, teenagers, thin-looking boys stoic behind
blacked-out shades and smiling Japanese girls busily snap-
ping pictures of the boats, one another and the huge gulls
unfurling for the sky, images that probably felt essential to
the moment but which would mean less than little in the
colder light of a month's or a year's perspective.

Rather than returning the way we'd come, Maggie
started the car east, towards Adrigole. The light thickened
further and every detail of the landscape seemed heightened. The ocean on our right fell into shades of cobalt and
then sky. A fatigue set in, one of those summer lulls that can
make simply breathing enough, and we sat at our respective windows, gazing out at the shapes and colours of the
world, no one saying much, no one really even thinking.
At Adrigole we turned north off the main road and followed a narrow byroad up through the Healy Pass between
the Slieve Miskish and Caha Mountains, stopping near the
summit in a small, chipped-gravel parking area so that we
could fully savour the views.

I've been many places in my life, but the Healy Pass felt

like we'd somehow strayed into another world. Wildness lay in every direction, something equal parts fearful and sublime, the kind of raw that made my blood itch. Layers of rugged granite mountainside, the casual filthy-white scatter of sheep flecking the distance, the tumbling ground a desperation of greenery, thick as pond-scum in parts, stewed to the colour of sand by sun and wind along the higher reaches, clogging the channels between the domineering rock.

Only Alison had thought to bring a camera, and she had us pose on the roadside, individually and then in various combinations, with the landscape spread out behind us. When it was her turn to stand with me, Maggie took over the camera and directed that we move closer, that Ali put her arm around my shoulder and I put mine around her waist. I have two copies of that photograph, our first together. One, enlarged to ten inches by twelve, hangs in our hallway. The other I keep tucked in my wallet. We appear so happy, comfortable in one another's company and so young. I see that more and more as time passes. Alison, slight beside me, looks beautiful in that simple pale blue cotton summer dress that shows off her shoulders and makes the world of her shape, and I seem fit and healthy, strong, in jeans and an old check-patterned shirt with the sleeves tucked to my elbows. We are looking at the camera and smiling but with a certain evident impatience, as if the photograph is costing us a precious second instead of preserving it forever. We had no way of knowing then that we'd get to share years of the life left to us, but that probably didn't stop us hoping. I think, though, that in the moment, as full to bristling with life as that moment was, all notion of a future seemed beyond us. There was then, and there was what had gone before. The rest was dreams.

I could not have imagined a more perfect afternoon. Looking back, because of the dense nature of the light and, even more so, the way in which time seemed to turn in on itself, it had the quality of a delusion, too idyllic to be true. We had whole other lives spinning around us, demanding our attention, but I felt removed, shielded from all of that and safe in the company I'd found. Alison felt the same, I think. I can remember the way the air tasted, and the feel of her body warm beside me and so alive through the cotton of her dress, so full of a beating heart. We were sharing some essence of ourselves, and I only know that it was as good as I'd felt in the longest time.

The road down the other side of the pass was slow and full of folds, each turn opening up the land below and ahead of us to a different and unexpected view. We continued on to Lauragh, where we once more met the ocean, then followed the coastline west again to Allihies. The day felt compressed, and we watched the landscape from the rolled-down windows and talked in low, disconnected voices, making easy, pleasant conversation as a way to help pass the miles. Broaching subjects of little consequence: the most famous people we'd met, our favourite films and film stars, the five albums we couldn't live without, the five songs that best defined us as people, as if songs alone could do that. Liz revealed an affection for the medieval strangeness of Pentangle and Steeleye Span, and songs like 'Gaudete'; Maggie claimed to have seen Ronnie Wood of the Rolling Stones in one of the duty-free shops at Heathrow, though she'd been too shy to approach him for an autograph; and Alison surprised us by offering *Smokey and the Bandit* as her all-time favourite film, not because she considered it the greatest ever made – though it had, she said, an undeniable and for her irresistible charm – but because of how much pleasure it had given her father. He'd died of a brain haemorrhage when she was young, just seven years old, and she could recall little about him but had a vivid memory of huddling up beside him on the couch and feeling shivers of happiness at the sound and raw vibration of his laughter whenever Jackie Gleason hit the screen.

She cried whenever she watched it now, she said, laughing with embarrassment at having revealed more of herself than she'd intended, and she nodded in acknowledgement of my attention and then turned her face away and set to studying the passing hillsides.

After this, we lapsed again into a sleepy silence, and by five o'clock had arrived back at the cottage. While Liz and Alison lingered outside to enjoy the warm air and the view over the ocean, I helped Maggie to haul out some chairs.

In the kitchen I caught her watching me, a smirk causing her eyes to shine.

'What?'

'Nothing. Just, you and Alison. I'm not imagining the spark, am I?'

'You imagine everything,' I said, wanting to be annoyed.

She lifted one of the kitchen chairs and struggled towards the back door. 'Did you kiss her yet?' she asked, without turning, just as she was about to step outside.

'Let's make a deal. I tell you to mind your own business and you agree.'

'But this is my business. Since I'm the one stirring the pot. And where's the harm in a bit of friendly advice?'

I sighed. 'Give it a rest, Maggie. It's too hot for your games.'

'Well, just don't wait too long. That's all I'm saying.'

We sat around until it was almost too dark to see, drinking, though not to excess, having already burnt ourselves out the night before, sticking with beer and enjoying the ease of one another's company. Dinner was two large pizzas, cooked from frozen and eaten from our laps, a plain cheese shared between Maggie and Liz, and a hot pepperoni and mushroom that I split with Alison, and at some point in the evening, at Liz's suggestion, we took ourselves down for a stroll on the beach. In what little of the day remained, the sand was hot and the water, when we kicked off our shoes and waded in shin-deep, felt warm and inviting. Maggie wanted us to swim, even though we had no bathing suits, but Alison's shyness won out. I caught her glance, and made her blush by smiling in a way that she couldn't have been expected to know yet was an expression of helplessness, and I suppose I would have gone along with the fun but was equally glad, and relieved, to be spared the ordeal.

Dusk suited the ocean. The sun slipped away, having burnt the sky with the colours of heat and turning the water to blood and blackness. The only sounds were the horseplay of Liz and Maggie splashing one another and the accompaniment of their high, raucous laughter, and away to the east the first constellation fell into view, a silvery dusting, nameless to us, that kept its own order and had been climbing the night forever. I came out of the water and moved a few paces up along the beach. Alison stood a little apart from the others, and when she turned and waved to me I raised a hand, smiled and waved back. My jeans were rolled up to my knees and I'd unbuttoned my shirt, and the air felt good against my body.

And then, once more, away to my left in the direction of the rocks, a flicker of whiteness snagged my peripheral vision. My heart quickened. The reefs lay empty before me, but secretive. I started towards them, then stopped. Alison must have been watching me, because she came up out of the water, calling my name.

'Mike? What is it? Did you see something again?'

I shrugged. 'I don't know. A movement, I think. It's probably nothing. Too much beer. I suppose I'm just not used to all this stillness.'

Her face was very close to mine, her eyes black and glassy. I could feel her breath on my skin. I didn't plan it, I just leaned in and kissed her. Not thinking, but unable to help myself. And far from trying to resist, she closed her eyes and her hand slipped into mine and she came against me, slight and delicate but with an unexpected assurance, and I felt myself drawn deep into her darkness. There was a sense of free fall, with no expectation of the interrupting ground. I let go and the seconds lost their way, and when we finally stepped apart I was surprised that so little had changed on the surface of the world. I could feel the banging of my heart all the way up into my throat, and I drew a deep breath and let it go, feeling it quiver through me and explode away, but twenty, thirty paces down the strand, Maggie and Liz, oblivious to our seismic movements, kept on with their splashing game amid the squeals for mercy and revenge, and the night itself had not advanced an inch against the plummy dusk. I wanted to speak but Ali's hand was still in mine, our fingers entwined, and when I glanced again in the direction of the reefs, there was nothing to see.

'A gull,' she murmured, for the second time in mere hours. Returning to its nest, no doubt, after a day spent scavenging the shoreline, a lone white flash settling for the night among the rocks. I nodded agreement, but turned us both away so that I wouldn't have to glimpse it again.

*

'So, tell us, Michael. Would you say you're in the habit of seeing ghosts?'

Maggie was on her knees in the centre of the room,

lighting candles. Every time she struck a fresh match her face bloomed momentarily yellow into view, but when the match went out, usually to a puff of breath, she seemed engulfed by the night, sucked back down into its abyss. The candles remained lit, but in few enough numbers yet to properly penetrate the dark, and only a suggestion of her features lingered until the next match flared, the lines of her face holding largely as a memory.

Her tone was old ground, a stilted, good-natured mocking that played to her audience yet knew better than to fully abandon its own doubt. I sat back in the armchair and pretended to consider the question. We were all tired and happy after a long day, and she'd already cracked the seal on the first of two bottles of Jameson bought earlier from the off-licence in Castletownbere, half-filling four water glasses despite our dutiful protestations.

I didn't really mind being teased.

'I wouldn't say in the habit, no. But being around artists so much, I'm certainly no stranger to the unusual. Or, let's face it, the downright weird. So, I've seen some things. I don't think I'd call them ghostly, though. And I'm not sure I'd call this ghostly, either.'

'Describe it.'

I studied the glow of the candles. The elongated yellow

stillness of the flames added atmosphere and encouraged an almost prayerful calm but at the same time seemed to lend the dark a greater density, emphasising the blind corners. Beside me, barely an arm's reach away, Alison sat curled up on the sofa, her legs tucked beneath her, most of the weight of her body leaning leftwards onto one elbow, and the armrest, watching me. I didn't have to turn to feel her gaze or to sense the hint of a smile that had gained such a new and comfortable permanence on her mouth.

'I'm not sure I can,' I said. 'This morning I really did think it was a person, a girl or a young woman. Because it wouldn't have been unreasonable to find someone on the rocks. But looking back, I don't know, it doesn't feel quite real. It's as if I have all the pieces but they won't fit together. And then, tonight, all I got was a glimpse, a white movement gone before I could properly even focus. I'm sure the dusk didn't help, or maybe that was the reason I saw anything at all.' I shrugged. 'Like Alison said, it was probably just a gull. Or my mind playing tricks.'

From outside, the approaching sound of footsteps interrupted our chat. We knew it was only Liz, but a certain disquiet layered our silence, which most likely had to do with how heavy the night felt. After a few seconds, she came through the door, carrying a white plastic bag shaped to the large flat squareness of a board game or an old LP record.

Maggie was still on her knees on the floor, the flesh of her upturned face shining now like honey in the glow of the small surrounding flames.

'Where'd you go? I poured you a drink.'

'Oh, thanks. I just needed something out of the car.'

'You shouldn't have gone up alone, Liz. Jesus, it's so dark. And that path still needs surfacing. You could easily have fallen or turned an ankle.'

Liz raised the plastic bag. 'I remembered that I'd brought this from home, to help us while away the hours. And of course I knew there'd be alcohol involved. But I must say, the candles are the perfect touch.'

'What is it?' Maggie asked, reaching for the bag. 'Snakes and Ladders?'

I leaned forward in my chair and watched her uncover a stiff white sheet of cardboard. The neat black block-capital letters of the alphabet had been laid out by hand across the centre of the sheet in two slightly arcing lines, giving the effect of a stretched and colourless rainbow, and directly beneath, following the same sweep, a row of numbers running from one to nine and finishing with a zero. In the top left corner, Liz had drawn a circle of sun with spider-leg rays alongside the word 'Yes', and in the top right a crescent moon and the word 'No'.

'It's a Ouija board,' I said. 'I've only seen these in films. You made this?'

'A few nights ago. I thought we could have some fun with it. Old houses are stuffed to splitting with memories, and it'd be a shame to waste the opportunity.'

I drained my whiskey. I can't say why I felt so uneasy. I'm not sure, even at that point, that I'd have described myself as a complete non-believer, but neither would I have come anywhere near fitting even the most relaxed definition of religious. Life, from what I'd seen of it, was complicated enough without adding superstition to the stew. But every time I closed my eyes I was back on the beach, alone this time, in the first of the morning light, a grim and colourless dawn caught between seasons. And I was walking towards the rocks.

'I've heard of them,' Alison said, 'but I've always been wary of using one.'

She rose from the couch and began to clear the table. I watched her, trying to read her thoughts, but couldn't decide whether what I was seeing was anxiety or excitement. It was one of those airless nights and the room felt warm. I undid a button on my shirt, and when that did not suffice I got up and went to stand for a moment in the doorway. Outside, apart from the spray of light from an unseen moon ribbing what had to be the ocean, blackness dominated. I stood there, breathing deeply of the dark, tasting its salt and chlorophyll sweetness, and didn't turn until Maggie called out to me. The others were already seated on three sides of the table, the board laid out flat between them. I went after the open bottle before joining them, facing Liz, with Alison on my left and Maggie to my right.

'So, what do we do?'

Liz had the board facing her. A small spiral notepad, a pen and one of the shimmering candles lay beside her right hand. She placed a shot glass upturned on the centre of the board.

'There's nothing to it. We each just put a finger on the glass, like this, and I'll ask the questions. Hopefully we'll get a response.'

'Hopefully?' Alison gave up a cough of laughter, a jarring sound that hit, then fell just as suddenly away.

'Well, there are no guarantees, of course. But if this sort of thing works at all then it'll surely work here. The west coast is full of places like this, homes left to ruin after the Famine hit and the population either fled or just died out. A lot of the bodies weren't even properly buried. They simply lay where they fell until time and the ground swallowed them up. The past must be thick as tar in these parts.'

My heartbeat had quickened. I sucked down whiskey from my glass and held the final dregs on my tongue. The flavours of the land filtered up through the heat, a mineral sting of dirt and turf and clean water. A weight settled in my throat and the high part of my chest. I smiled to myself, but only for the benefit of the others, in case any of them happened to be watching. Then I poured myself another shot.

Across the table, Liz closed her eyes and asked, in a whisper, that we do the same. We each reached out, placed an index finger on the base of the upturned glass, and shut our eyes. Something about that deep and sudden closed-off darkness, perhaps in combination with the alcohol I'd consumed, did something unpleasant to me, brought on a vertigo state that set me in some inner way off-kilter. I held my breath, which seemed to help, but not quite enough, and after a minute or so I gave up.

The candlelight seemed stronger now. The others kept the stillness of standing stones, dutiful, at least on a surface level, in their compliance, ready and open to some trance state. But their clenched mouths were braced, their nerves wired against the least touch or sound. I came within half a second of slapping the table. But I held back. Their anxiety was real. Instead, I focused on the glass in the dead centre of the table, and waited. I think, looking back, that I knew something would happen.

'Are there any spirits present?' Liz asked at last, pitching the words a clear tone at least above what was usual for her. Beside me, the hint of a smile, most likely shaped by fear, creased the corners of Alison's lips. 'If there is anyone here, please give us a sign. Make a tapping sound, speak through one of us, help us to move this glass. Please give us a sign that you can hear us.'

'Do you feel that?' Maggie whispered. She opened her eyes and stared at the glass, then raised her gaze, with pleading, to Liz.

'That's Mike.'

'It's not.' To prove my innocence I raised my hand.

'I still feel it. Like a vibration.'

I touched the glass again. She was right. A tremor, barely perceptible, as if it were catching the hum of an almost-tuned radio signal.

'What is that?'

'There's something here,' Liz said, her voice thick with the pure thrilled air of dread. 'I think it's drawing energy from us. Just wait.'

The vibration deepened. We all felt it. The glass was cold to the touch but its resonance crept slowly up my arm, a little bit like the pins and needles sensation of blood rushing back to a limb after a period of prolonged numbness. Then, by degrees, the glass set to quivering, and I watched, transfixed, we all did, until that alone became the measure of time and everything else ceased to matter. Beside me, very softly, Alison began to cry. She made no sound apart from a slight disruption to her breathing. The tracks of her tears gleamed in the candlelight. I reached for her and took her free hand, not caring what the others thought, and she wove her fingers between mine in a way that linked our arms inside the elbow. The skin of her palm was cool and dry, familiar still from our morning on the beach, and for just an instant, for me, the glass lessened in importance. Gradually, though, its trembling intensified. Within a minute it had started, quite visibly, to rock.

'Christ. It's actually moving.'

'Just take it easy, everyone.'

'Is this real?' asked Maggie. 'We should be filming this.'

Liz raised her free hand, demanding silence, and again lifted her voice to its peculiar new pitch.

'Who is here with us? Please try to identify yourself.' She looked around, as if expecting to see something. 'Use our energy to spell out your name.'

Everything stopped. We held our breath and glanced at one another. Maggie began to laugh.

'Funny, Mike. You're a real hoot.'

'I told you,' I said, with more force than I'd intended. I felt angry, for no good reason. And I knew it, but couldn't seem to help myself. 'It wasn't me.'

'Fine. Liz then.'

'Wait.'

'What is it?'

'It's moving again,' Alison whispered. 'Oh Christ, I think I'm going to be sick.'

Steadily then, the glass began to slide across the cardboard, slipping in apparently random fashion among the letters. My view of the board was inverted, which made it difficult to follow the pattern with any real accuracy, but Alison, beside me, who had a slightly better view, tightened her grip on my hand. I could hear the wet tear of her breath and then a constricting gasp when the glass again came to rest. Across the table, Liz, mumbling to herself, scribbled down the letters on her notepad. Then she raised the pad, tilted it so that it caught the sheen of candlelight, and considered for a moment what she'd written.

'It must be in Irish,' she said, and let out a long, unsteady sigh. 'I think it says, *An Máistir*. The Master.'

Alison's crying intensified. 'Oh, Jesus. I told you. This is dangerous. We need to stop before something goes wrong.'

'Don't worry,' Liz said, trying for the sort of reassurance that I could see, even in the darkness, she did not quite feel. 'I've done this before. We're fine. Really. Nothing can go wrong. We're free to stop at any time.'

'Then I'd like to stop now.'

'Ali, please,' said Maggie. 'Let's just give it a few more minutes. Then we'll stop if you still want to. But it's just a bit of fun.'

'It's not my idea of fun,' Alison said, but she reached out and returned the tip of her left index finger to the glass. After a moment of hesitation, the rest of us did the same. Immediately, the glass began to vibrate, rocking slightly from side to side, then again set to drifting across the board, the movement slow, casual, hitting letters in flurries and stopping for seconds at a time. Twice or three times I was certain that it had finished, but then it would stir once more and continue on its crawl.

'Well? What did he say?'

Liz studied her notepad. 'It's difficult to tell where one word begins and another ends. I thought it'd make more sense than this. When I've done it before it's always been much easier to follow. But this is in Irish, and even at school mine was never much better than terrible. As far as I can make out, it says, '*An bhfuil cead agam teacht isteach?*' which I think means, 'Can I come in?' Or words to that effect. Well, that's what it does mean, but something like that would be a literal translation. I think he's asking for permission to join us.'

She looked at me, and I could see her fear but also a kind of electric delight, an excitement that the candle's yellow glow stretched and sharpened towards something manic.

'Yes,' she said, raising her voice and lifting her eyes towards the ceiling. 'You may enter. Welcome, Master.'

For almost a minute, there was no sound. And then we became aware of a noise coming from across the room, in one of the corners. Small at first, barely noticeable, but growing steadily more hectic. A rustling sound, like that of a small rodent scrabbling through fallen leaves. Of the three candles on the table, one, alongside Maggie, guttered and went out. A squeal jerked loose from her, followed by a gasp of embarrassed laughter. 'Sorry,' she whispered, which for no reason I could explain, made me smile, too.

'Did you live in this house?' Liz asked, ignoring us and the noise, keeping her focus, and beneath our fingertips the glass drifted towards the board's upper left corner, hit 'Yes' and fell back a few inches.

'Did you die here?'

Again, it moved to 'Yes' before drawing back.

'How did you die?'

Now, instead of moving forward, the glass began to rock, quickening to violence.

'Stop,' Alison pleaded. 'We're making him angry. We have to stop.'

'How did you die?' Liz repeated.

The glass was alive now beneath our combined touch. It rattled madly on the board, then all at once stopped dead. We each held our breath, until the stillness was torn open by a loud thump on the ceiling directly above us, like the landing of something heavy from a height, and the glass began to crawl again, a long sweep across to T, back to E, to A, to D. We looked at Liz, but she could only shrug. Her eyes were wide and yellow in the candlelight, and her lips moved in silence to the word, the letters first and then the whole. Seconds passed. Then, again, the glass moved, T, E, A, D. T, E, A, D. T, E, A, D. Slowly, then quickening, over and over until our gazes anticipated a kind of pattern. T, E, A, D.

'For Christ's sake,' Maggie said, her voice a husk. 'Ask him what *tead* means.'

The glass stopped in mid-repetition. And so slowly that

each letter seemed underlined, it started to trace a new direction. R, O, P, E.

'Oh, Jesus.'

'Rope. You committed suicide?'

Again the glass slid towards 'Yes'.

'Why?'

Gan aon bhia. Lack of food. *Ocras.* Hunger. Even with the night's cloying heat, I felt numb. I watched the glass, trying to comprehend what exactly I was seeing. Logic suggested that someone could easily have been manipulating the situation, but I didn't suspect Maggie and it certainly wasn't Alison. Liz seemed the most obvious candidate, if someone had to be. History, as we had come to realise, captivated her, and she'd already made passing reference to her interest in the occult, a fascination bordering perhaps on the obsessive but which she seemed to consider quite natural, since poetry was, she said, in its purest sense little more than a channelling anyway, an alchemy that helped solidify the ephemeral. Yeats knew it. So did Blake, and Shelley, and Donne, and Ted Hughes. I'd have liked to believe that this was all part of a game for her, but one look at her determined flame-yellowed face convinced me otherwise.

For the next few minutes, she persisted with her questions. The responses came slowly, often in broken sentences but at least now in English, though there were still instances of occasional relapse, missteps confined mainly to single words. She scratched down each message and attempted to decipher its meaning from the few clustered letters, but even when delivered in a language we could all understand the full sense of these words was mostly lost to us. *Teach them. Pray.* A name, Crom, which, according to Liz, referred to an early pagan deity.

Then Maggie began to speak. Her voice seemed full of air and had a low, considered hush that made the sound of rain on glass, and was recognisably hers but also, in some peculiar way, not. She sat on my right side but had turned partially from the table and become fixated on a point of distance somewhere behind and beyond Liz, though the darkness in that direction was absolute. The flames of the two remaining candles bounced and jogged, their glow tormenting her semi-profile, pulling at the stripes of shadow, elongating the clean planes of her skin.

'He lived here,' she said. 'This was his home. And he hanged himself in this room. From these rafters. For ten days he'd eaten nothing but grass. Up until then the people around here had survived on rats, insects, any birds that they could catch. Other things, too.'

'What other things?'

'The blight had come and then come back, and the first year was terrible but only the beginning. The shellfish were lost when the ocean brought a red tide, and the second year the herring stayed north, out of reach of the boats. So there was nothing. And it was bad for everyone. A mile over, towards Allihies, a fisherman's wife was lost in birthing. One of the women saved the child through butchery, but it was born small and seven weeks early and died that first night. The fisherman sent the woman out, then blocked the door and set fire to the thatch. The house took almost an hour to go. There were three more children in the house and those who had come down to see said they never woke, that they were already dead from smoke before the flames reached them. And the fisherman stood at the half-door, staunch as a tree, gazing out into the darkness, until the roof came down around him. In the days after, the neighbours raked through the embers, collecting what could be salvaged.'

'Maggie?' Liz asked, trying to remain calm. 'What are you saying? How do you know all this?'

Maggie's stare never left the distance. When she was not speaking we could all hear the papery rustle of her breathing. 'I don't know,' she murmured. 'It's just here, in my head. Pictures, words. I can see it. It's difficult to explain. I feel as if it's being whispered to me. I don't hear a voice, not exactly, but I feel it. I know what's being said.'

We were all still touching the upturned glass. For now, it had stopped moving, but nothing was finished.

'He kept school down in one of the back acres, sometimes down on the beach. The children came from as far away as Cahirkeen in the north and Knockroe to the south. Men and women, too, as things began to deteriorate. He taught them to read and add up, but mostly he instructed them in older ways of worship. The priests had come, of course, generations of them, and they'd thrived during the better times when prayers never had to be more than easy words. They were tolerated but couldn't quite belong, and they never penetrated the fabric because the stories they told had no grounding here. This land had its own gods, ancient when the likes of Christ were young. These gods controlled the sun and the tide and the seasons, and they were cruel and vengeful to disobedience but generous to loyalty, protecting those who knew how to properly ask. And the people needed instruction, especially once the potatoes turned putrid in the fields and everything stopped growing. They needed to make amends for what had been abandoned.'

'How bad was it?'

'Bad. People began dying on the roadside, in ditches. On a still day, or if the wind was coming from the wrong direction, you could hear the keening for miles. Early in the second year, he killed a girl. A child, sixteen, seventeen years old. He'd taken her away from the group and led her down onto the beach. She wore a torn smock and hadn't eaten in more than three days. They held hands on the path and across the sand towards the rocks, where no one could see them, and when he made her naked and bent her over the first low outcropping her ribs and backbone stood against her pale skin like the ridges in a ploughed field. She cried out when he entered her, a small, deep, destroyed moan, and he felt her break in a warm gout, and through what followed she gripped the rock with one hand for balance and held her head in the other, gagging with pain and imploring of him to stop. But he didn't stop, couldn't. He kept on until his own control snapped, and then he slumped against her, breathing deep, shuddering breaths, and her body held beneath him, a delicately carved thing but cold and still as something already dead except for the enduring hum of her crying. He kissed the filthy sweep of her neck, the skin coated with sweat and dirt and pocked raw by the stabbing of ticks, then ran his fingers into and against the spill of her tangled hair, jerked her head up twenty inches and before she could resist or even breathe to scream smashed her face five or six times back down into the reefs. She died almost instantly but he didn't stop until she was ruined, and then he smeared clots of her blood into the skin of his own face, chest and groin, cradled the body in his arms and waded out into the ocean. It was a sacrifice, part of the ritual, the sowing of a seed, the reaping of a life, and an attempt to sate Manannán, almighty of the sea, and the Cailleach, and Crom Cruach, the thunder-crack, the god of day, of the sun.'

I wanted to be sick. I wanted to get up from the table and just run, in any direction as long as it would take me away from here, and from this. But I didn't. I couldn't move. And neither could anyone else. We sat there, listening, numb with growing horror, while the words came like rain and the story built and gushed.

They all knew. Everyone knew, even the family of the girl, the father and sister she'd left behind. What he had done, and why. And that he had done it for them. Worse, they'd all colluded. They helped select her, and, by turning away, by sitting in the acre in a silent huddle, studying the sky or the dirt but never one another, they'd granted him permission to do what he claimed and assured them was necessary. But a month passed, and then a second, and nothing changed. The anger of the gods didn't abate, and no prayers were heard. Maybe their faith had been allowed lie too long fallow. By October, he himself had taken ill. He'd started eating grass, as many did, just to feel his mouth full again, and spent desperate days hunched in pain, his shrunken stomach knotted with cramp. There was talk, just a whisper but with a ring of truth about it, that further north, in parts of Mayo and Galway, areas where the blight had wreaked even greater havoc and where even the grass had ceased to grow, some had taken to eating their dead. The ones who spoke of this, and those who heard, shook their heads and tried to force the thought away, but the natural abhorrence for such acts had softened, dictated by a deeper ache.

On the fifth day after falling ill, he saw his wife at the window. Áine. She had passed several years earlier, during their second year of marriage, taken by yellow fever. Back then, he'd spent most of his days out on the water, waiting for the return of spring, and he should have been with her because he'd known she was bad, though not how bad, not that her condition would prove so quickly fatal. She died alone, sweating her heart to stillness in a bed that he later had to haul outside and burn, and for a long time after, months at least, perhaps even as long as a year, he continued to see her everywhere. Then, gradually, she seemed to fade from his life, and in those final days, until she again started appearing to him, he could hardly even recall her face. He was on the floor, slumped in a corner of the empty room, and lifted his head to find her at the window, looking in, watching. He felt only a sense of calm at the sight of her, maybe even relief. And what struck him was not the paleness of her complexion but the familiar brittleness of her shape, her slender shoulders, the narrow hips. She was not smiling but there seemed no sadness about her, either. She was simply waiting, as she had waited so often in life, gazing out over the ocean for the first hint of his return. And following this visit, she came back often, standing in the doorway as he lay down on the floor to sleep, accompanying him in the mornings and during the last of the light when he trawled the beach in search of a bite to eat, even the least morsel – a crab, a mussel, dead carrion, a snarl of kelp, anything. She never spoke, because they had no need for words. Her expression was placid, unchanging, a mask of infinite patience. Waiting, he'd come to know, for realisation to take full hold.

As the days built and passed, he grew increasingly weak, until eventually even standing presented too great a challenge. That final morning, he stumbled outside into the rain, fell to his knees in a corner of the field nearest the house and ate what grass he could force into his mouth. His teeth had begun to fall out, the gums receding in a way that turned everything loose, and he lay for hours on that patch of ground, through into the afternoon, on his side, helpless, with the juice running green from his nose and broken lips. Waves of cramp kept tearing him from the stupor of a punch-drunk sleep, the violent purge of his stomach convulsing, giving up its yellow acids and, in ropes of blood, its lining. Sometimes, when he could force open his eyes, he saw the disc of sun like the hole of a musket shot at half-height in the sky, muted to opalescence by a skin of cloud. But more often the cloud banked itself in layers so dense that there was nothing at all but the unbroken greyness, and the threat of further rain. And then, on towards evening, he saw her again, standing just out of reach, and as she moved before him he moved too, struggling first to his knees and then his feet, and following her inside, surrendering at last to what he had to do.

'He'd prepared for this. He had already hung the rope and tied the noose. All that remained now was its execution.'

Maggie's words guided us, but I found that I could also picture it, as clearly as if it were playing out in real time before me. I could see him climb, with the little strength left to him, up onto the chair and then the table, bring himself to its edge, put his head through the loop, and draw away the few inches of slack, twisting it so that the rope's fibres bit into the flesh of his throat and the big knuckle of knot settled heavily just behind and below his left ear. So that the end would be quick. So that even if the neck failed to give, the jugular almost certainly would. He'd seen men hang before, and knew the way. He closed his eyes to spare himself the sight of the window that lay ahead, the blanched filter of the light spilling through the narrow, unshuttered gape with its boast of the world beyond and the small, good things that world still possessed. But the new pitch blackness put up an instant, nauseous challenge to his balance and when he opened his eyes again, Áine was standing there, just inside the window, her shape diffusing the light but not stemming it. And as he leaned forward from the table's edge towards her, she reached out her arms and for the first time in half a lifetime revealed the teeth inside her smile.

The candles guttered again. Beside me, Alison was weeping hard. She gripped my hand tightly and from the darkness asked in a tiny, fractured voice that we please stop now. Across from us, Liz nodded and tipped the glass onto its side. Her eyes were yellow fire in the light of the remaining candles, and I could see that she was crying, too. I got up and switched on the light, and brought the fresh bottle back to the table. We started in on it without talking, none of us knowing, I suppose, quite what to say.

There was something blocked about that whiskey-fuelled aftermath. What had occurred lay around us like the taint of pepper in the air, a slow poison that once tasted cannot be easily forgotten. Alison gripped my hand and announced that under no circumstances would she sleep alone, that she'd make do with a blanket and an armchair, propriety be damned. She kept seeing it, she said. Over and over. Her mind was scarred with it. And she couldn't understand why it was so vivid. Maggie was the one who'd spoken the words, but why had we all been able to see? And on my right, Maggie nodded, but seemed vague, as if she had not yet all the way returned from wherever it was that she'd been taken. She held her glass in both hands but only now and then remembered to drink, and her eyes retained a particular kind of stare, the look of having glimpsed too much, and of having been invaded.

★

An hour or so later, the house had fallen silent. I'd surrendered the sofa, which seemed like the chivalrous thing to do, and helped Alison arrange her bed, announcing that I was happy enough to settle for the armchair. And, in truth, I didn't at all mind sitting up, and was not yet done with the whiskey. After a while, Liz led Maggie away to the bedroom, and for several minutes the soft mumble of their voices came through the wall and insinuated the air of the living room with a vague second frequency. I listened only because the sound was there, but the words themselves were shapeless, indecipherable.

Alison slipped out of her dress and hurried beneath her quilt in just her underwear. I kept my eyes averted without needing to be asked yet still somehow caught a fleeting glimpse, a flash of body. She noticed, I think, but said nothing. And from the sofa, snug to her chin beneath the duvet, she watched me openly as I stood and set about unbuttoning my shirt.

'It's so warm tonight. Do you think it'd be all right to leave the window open?'

'I think so,' I said. 'But let me get the light first. Otherwise the place will swarm with flies.'

I folded my shirt, laid it across the back of one of the kitchen chairs, and slipped on a T-shirt before stepping out of my jeans. But when I switched off the light we again felt plunged into something worse than darkness. She gasped, a tiny helpless sound, against the immensity of it, and then a silence opened up beyond that, and held for what seemed like a long time. I settled in the armchair, sipped at the last of my whiskey, and had finally started contemplating the idea of sleep when she cleared her throat and asked, in a whisper unbearably small with upset, if I'd sit with her for a while, if I'd hold her. I put down my glass and came to her, groping my way in the dark, and when I opened my embrace for her to slip inside she pressed against me so hard that I could feel the banging of her heart, the hot vibrato of her breath against the underside of my chin, the burn of her cheeks still feverish with earlier tears. We held that position for as long as we could, until it began to feel awkward, and then we lay down together, not anticipating anything except comfort and reassurance.

Dawn's breaking surprised me. I felt the shift of the light and opened my eyes. It was still early, maybe five o'clock, and everything was still. Alison lay asleep against my chest. My usual habit on waking is to rise immediately, without thought as to the time, but this morning I resisted the urge. Caged within the darkness, the events of the night before had lost their definition. Something had certainly happened, we'd gone too far with the game, but already the edges were beginning to fray. Night holds its own reality, one that boasts ample room for monsters. By contrast, the stillness of this grey-breaking dawn was perfect.

'You slept.'

Alison shifted her head onto my shoulder. She gazed up at me, without smiling. The hem of the duvet had slipped to the small of her back, and in that fragile first light her eyes had the dark, dull sheen of pewter. She looked serious and suddenly young, a girl of nineteen or twenty, innocent still of the world and afraid of everything it offered.

'I think so,' I said, and, without planning to, brought my mouth to hers. For the time of a slow kiss everything stopped and there was only us, pinned together, unexpectedly happy. We remained like that, disturbing the contented silence as little as possible and even then limiting our talk to long sighs and whispers, the words soft as dust and almost as shapeless, until eventually we were roused by the first sounds of movement from the bedroom next door. I got up and settled again in the armchair, and a few minutes later Maggie announced herself with a small tapping on the room door.

'Everyone awake? Tell me if I'm disturbing anything?'

'Come on in,' I said. 'We're decent enough.'

She pushed through into the room and considered us. 'Pity,' she mumbled, then went to the window and looked out. The sky had already softened, and a light dew had set the long stringy grass of the back fields to shining. Only the ocean looked fully dark.

I got up from the armchair and slipped on my jeans. 'I'll make coffee,' I said, and went through to the kitchen and lifted the pot onto the range. When I came back into the doorway, Maggie had perched herself on the edge of the sofa and was leaning over Alison, murmuring something that made both of them smile. They lifted their eyes, and Maggie considered me once more, this time with mocking amusement, scrutinising the stretch between my face and bare feet and slowly back again. I waited, not reacting, my demeanour holding to a game of calm, and when the coffee began to percolate I returned to the kitchen, lined up three mugs and poured, and only then allowed myself an easy breath.

Breakfast was scrambled eggs, slices of locally produced black pudding, slightly warmed soda bread and more coffee. I cooked, happy that the familiar routine could put me at ease. Liz sat quietly at the table. When I set a plate before her, she raked the tines of her fork through the eggs, ploughing straight and then cross patterns in the yellow pulp, and whispered to none of us in particular that her head felt as if someone had been swinging at her with an axe. I couldn't help but smile. She took a bite of soda bread, chewed and swallowed, then gave up and settled back with her coffee. 'Christ,' she went on. 'What was I thinking? And when I did finally get to sleep, the nightmares hardly let up the whole night. That's it, I'm done with whiskey, for good and ever. Last night was absolutely the last time.'

I was surprised at my own appetite. The eggs revived me, and the coffee lit a fire. Everything was so fresh – the eggs, the milk, the bread – and perhaps because of the morning air's clean snap, or because of what Alison had awakened in me, every taste felt heightened. I would have liked a final walk on the beach, but it was already somehow nine o'clock, and there was just no time. My flight wasn't until three, but I needed to be checked in and so had to allow the guts of two and a half hours for the drive back. Three, if I were to hit traffic, which was unlikely, especially for a Sunday, but still possible. So I settled instead for standing at the back door, breathing the flavours and taking in the shades. You could already feel the heat, a promise of what the day would hold, and the air hardly moved, except when physically disturbed. A part of me, a small part, began to wish that I'd allowed myself a longer visit.

'Thanks for coming,' Maggie said, joining me in the doorway and then easing me a step outside. She slipped an arm around my waist and brought herself snug against me. 'I hope you had a nice time.'

I kissed the top of her head. 'Knock it off,' I said.

'What?'

'You know what. You always know. The insinuations. For once in your life, stop interfering.'

'It's a perfectly innocent thing to say.'

'You're a long stone's throw from innocent.'

'I'm offended.'

'Well, the truth often offends.'

'I suppose. Anyway, I just wanted to let you know that I'm happy for you. I really am. Alison's a sweetheart. And it's done you the world of good. Both of you.'

'Go ahead,' I said. 'Mock. But nothing happened.'

She laughed. 'Relax, Mike. It's no big deal. Everyone is allowed a bit of happiness once in a while. Are you blushing?'

I stared at the ocean so that I wouldn't have to look at her. She'd always been able to read me like a news headline. Out in the distance, the water was deepening its colour, compressing more intently with every tidal pull from the shade of stone to that of unlit sapphire, and I could feel the insinuation of its crashing deep inside myself. A churning, as if I'd come to some brink and was about to be pulled in, as if I needed that. Dandelions and tufts of flowering ragwort speckled the field before us, bright as sovereigns and small suns among the scant scrub, and I knew that I was seeing the very things that artists saw, but yet again in too evolved a way, the detail but not the greater effect, and not the significance of all that lay beneath.

'Will you be all right here? Alone, I mean?'

'Are you offering your protection?'

'Come on.'

She hugged me tight. 'Thanks for worrying about me, Mike. And for asking. But I'll be fine. As soon as I saw this place something moved in me. This is where I belong. It's as if I can think more clearly here, or maybe that I don't need to think at all. I'll be able to paint again now. I know I will. And that's what really matters, at least for me. Without the desire for that, I'm nothing. I'm a shell. There's no meaning to my life.' For a second, a smile broke the surface, and she sighed with deep and obvious contentment. 'I'd never thought about that before, you know? It took coming here to make me understand.'

'Well, you have my number if you need help. I mean it. I can be here in half a day.'

'I know. Thanks.'

We didn't discuss what had occurred the night before. It was in my mind to mention it, to ask where all that stuff had come from, and where she'd gone to while the words were flowing. But I held back. I told myself later that my silence on the subject was because whatever had lurked beneath the surface now seemed so diluted by the brilliance of a lovely new morning. But the truth was that a sting of fear still lingered with me, and it made me feel embarrassed and even, to a certain degree, ashamed. We all shared in that fear, and Alison, who'd been terrified nearly to hysteria, still carried the trauma of it in her expression. But I'd been the man in that room. I know that's an absurd train of thought, but to pretend otherwise would be less than honest. More was expected of me, if only from myself. Something had happened, the things Maggie had said were clearly not of her own making, but I couldn't bring myself to call her on it. We all think that we'll walk through walls for the people who matter most to us, that we'll willingly push ourselves against the muzzle of a gun for them. But we can't know. Not until the moment arrives. I loved Maggie like a sister, but when it came to doing the right thing I lacked the strength, and the courage. Instead, she and I stood in the doorway, in silence, arms around one another, watching the ocean.

Suddenly, I didn't want to go. The Ouija board was a mistake, but the rest of the weekend had been as close to perfect as any I'd known. The place, the company, the sense of escape, were all pleasures that I'd absorbed without conscious thought. But now that the time had come to give them up, I could feel the emptiness they'd leave behind. And it hurt more than I'd have believed possible. Work had dominated so much of my adult life, and it seemed ridiculous that I should feel such nostalgia for something I'd only briefly tasted. Yet the feelings couldn't be denied.

Just before leaving, I managed to manoeuvre a few minutes alone with Alison, but there was little we could think of to say, little I could promise beyond assuring her that I'd call as soon as I made it home. Now that we'd reached the moment of parting, we were both uncomfortable, and the embrace and kiss we shared was awkward and less than it might and probably should have been.

And then I went, and my memory of climbing the slope to where I'd parked the hired car has retained a startling clarity. I had on a clean shirt that was already beginning to dampen at the armpits and cling to the skin of my back, and for reasons I cannot quite explain I refused to let myself turn until reaching the road. I knew that Maggie was down there, waiting to wave me goodbye, and also that Alison had come outside to join her. The dirt of the path hinted at a mineral smell suggestively close to sulphur and had the dry, dead blackness of cinders except where mica poked through, causing it to glitter, and all the way to the top the strains of music accompanied me, seeping from the cottage through its open back door, piano and a voice that had lost its shape over distance but which I could recognise, largely because of the melody it carried, as something early Springsteen. When I did finally turn, the world off into the far distance had become majestic, a delusion familiar of any wild thing in its placid state. Maggie waved, and I raised a hand in my own so-long gesture. Because of a sense that I might glimpse something more than I was quite ready to see, I tried not to focus on any one detail other than the women, all three of them now, Liz having also wandered out to complete the huddle. Standing together, they looked lovely, full of youthfulness and life, but somehow vulnerable too, small against the world. They waved, and I could feel their smiles, and I waved back and counted seconds, then got into my car, let down the window, fired the engine and drove, tapping at the speed limit all the way, glad beyond words of the daylight.

Part II

The Dead House

Over the next several weeks, I let myself be consumed with work. A void of sorts had opened up within me, an emptiness that I knew no real way of filling, and so I compensated with long hours, wedging myself behind my desk and working the phones often late into the night, chasing deals both domestic and foreign, lining up exhibitions, closing sales. It was my coping mechanism, always has been. I left little room for life beyond the facts of business, apart from a few snatched days early in July, when Alison and I were able to enjoy a sweet if fleeting weekend rendezvous in a plush Edinburgh hotel after I'd been dragged northwards to promote a show for one of my artists.

Because I had slipped so far out of practice, and grown so used to the defensive wall I'd unknowingly built, it stunned me that we could be so natural with one another. But once the door closed behind us and we found ourselves alone together, the silences felt every bit as relaxed as the conversation. I've read that such easy stillness can count as one of the measures of love, though neither of us was anywhere near ready yet for a word as big as that. She stood at the foot of the bed, as comfortable as if she were alone in the room, emptying her small travel case in neat order and laying out the contents piece by piece. A change of clothes – skirt, blouse, sweater – a sleeveless white cotton nightgown, certain necessary toiletries, a slim pocket Berlitz guidebook to the city and a novel called *The Enigma of Arrival* marked roughly at a midway point with the green and white stub of an Aer Lingus boarding pass. I watched her from the grey-blue suede armchair, a wing-back that seemed built with precisely my shape in mind. An occasional breeze bothered the partially opened window's net curtains into small stirrings, and for those few minutes there was need for nothing else. I remember thinking that I'd never in my whole life been so happy. This was a realm of pleasure I'd believed preserved for others, for actors and rock stars and people who can live on the edge and act as though they actually belong there, untouched or undisturbed by the relentless combination jabs of guilt and duty. Not for the likes of me. Yet here I was, and I felt relaxed, in a way I'd rarely if ever known.

She finished unpacking, taking her time, then let her hair down and without so much as a hint of embarrassment began to undress. When she glanced at me, just the once, a tiny smile softened everything, and I understood that we had gone beyond the need for games. And later, in the yellowed dark of a city midnight, exhausted beyond sleep, we held to one another and talked in broken whispers. She and Maggie had spoken only once since the house-warming, she said. A call maybe ten days after, which had caught her one late afternoon at the gallery. Nothing too intense, just calling to say hello, and to chat a little. There were no problems that she could detect, apart from a kind of distance in Maggie's voice, but that could likely have been attributed to the line, or to her own imagination. I understood. Maggie often got that way when painting. Like she'd taken to living in a mire of fog. But other than that? Nothing particularly odd? No reason to worry? Because I'd had a couple of calls from her myself, her voice airily spinning from my answering machine after I'd gotten in late.

The first time, just checking in, nothing much to report except a snag with the plumbing, something minor but which was forcing her to bathe in an old tin basin that had come with the house. She'd held onto it after the clear-out, with the vague notion of maybe setting it up out front and filling it with flowers, and she'd had to spend the better part of half a day scrubbing with a wire brush just to get it back into some kind of usable condition. Still, it was more than worth the trouble, and there was something quite invigorating about dragging it into the living room and heating water in pots on the range. Sometimes she'd lie there in that water for an hour or more, she said, facing the window, watching the sun tumble into view on its way westward. And other than that, everything was fine. She'd been thinking also about maybe starting a garden, putting in some vegetables, a winter crop, even though it was probably a bit late in the season. Cabbage, turnips, carrots, a few drills of potatoes. The stuff of life, I thought, listening to her voice then and thinking about it afterwards. Reflections of contentment.

The second call came a couple of weeks later. Again, caught by the machine, it was something akin to a one-sided conversation, she asking questions that were left with no choice but to hang, and answering queries that I had no way of putting. Was everything all right with me? Had I done the right thing yet and let Alison make an honest if not quite decent man of me? Yes, she was painting again, I'd be glad to know. Well, sketching, and chancing some experimental and extremely loose watercolour work. Nothing serious, really just trying to get a good feel for the sky and the fall of the land. But she hoped, all going well, to have something saleable for me by the year's end. She wanted to paint the stone circle that she'd found in one of the fields above the cottage, and also the hills in twilight and the ocean in storm. In her mind, she said, she'd already begun. She could feel the lines of the work, the impact of the colours. She felt inspired. And the cottage? Yes, the cottage was fine, perfect, the joy of her life. On wet days the air turned white, and when the wind blew hard it made the sound of voices. So she had no shortage of company.

Alison's hair lay in sloey ropes across the pillow. She smiled, half asleep, while I inched my mouth along her collarbone and neck to her punctured but naked earlobe, and she opened her eyes wide and laughed when my hand slipped over her stomach and ribs and found the modest swell of her left breast. After that, and for the rest of the weekend, we talked only of other things, both of us unconsciously aware, I think, that any more on the subject of Maggie would have been too much and would quite possibly have ruined what we had going. For the next couple of days we strolled the city, absorbing the history, the culture, the sights, all the good things that the place had to offer. There were moments, real as flesh and bone, not only during the hours we spent in bed but also sitting together in some restaurant snug, feeding one another bites of lamb or braised beef, or just walking, holding hands, along the Royal Mile or around Greyfriars, when I found myself wanting this as a permanence in my life. A part of me knew that, because it was just a weekend, and because there was no hardship in such short-term surrender, I was not yet seeing the entire picture, but in the weeks after we'd both returned to our regular routines, the shining light of our Edinburgh experience did not abate. And it made me realise, or accept, that I'd been alone in every sense for far too long.

The phone became our tether. I'd call her most nights, unless either one of us had reason to be tied up, or else she'd call me. We'd chat then, clean through into the small hours, sharing the details of our day and considering, casually at first but, as the weeks passed, with increasing enthusiasm, just how good our time together had been, how great, actually, and how much we each longed for the chance to enjoy more of the same. The world felt empty now that we were apart. Briefly, we discussed the possibility of another weekend, some place close but nice, somewhere like Paris, and then I suggested that maybe she could just come to London and let me show her what a big city was really all about. She laughed and asked if I was talking about size, and I said of course I was, that size was everything when it came to cities and that we had it all here in London, the sights, the sounds, the history, even the shopping. All aspects of life, the glorious and the gruesome. And that's how it happens, I think, how relationships begin to define themselves as more than mere passing fancies. I started to see things from a new angle, and though at that point I still lacked the courage to put my thoughts into actual words, I'd already begun to consider how a future might play out for us, and just what it would take, just how much I was prepared to sacrifice, to make this something permanent.

The problem, the most pressing of the innumerable problems, was working open a window in what had become an extremely crammed schedule. At around this time, one of my artists picked up a major prize, for a piece that neither he nor I particularly rated as being properly representative of his talent but which broached a subject matter controversial enough to get itself noticed, and this drew an intense — if inevitably short-lived — flurry of media attention, an always desirable result but also incredibly time-consuming. For the greater part of June and on through into July, I had to spend hours every day handling requests for interviews and public appearances, speaking with newspapers, magazines, researchers from various television programmes, as well as entering into negotiations with a number of the major European and American galleries about possible exhibition space. Because the artist recognised this as a rare opportunity to etch himself a place in the social fabric, he agreed when I suggested that we move with caution and not let cash alone become the dictating factor. But such terrain was new to both of us, and we quickly discovered that some offers were simply too substantial to dismiss. And then, just as one frenzy began to wane, a second erupted. One of my newer clients, a dissident Chinese sculptor living the exiled Parisian attic existence, suddenly, on the back of a New York show that I'd arranged, fell into vogue. As a young artist, he'd been among those most fervently involved in his native country's pro-democracy movement, railing against the restrictions of the Cultural Revolution. He was present at the protests in Tiananmen Square, had helped design the placards and banners, witnessed the massacre and suffered imprisonment and worse for the part he'd played in one of his nation's dirtiest days. Following his release from captivity, after two and a half years of the most horrendous physical and psychological torture imaginable, one that included frequent beatings, sleep deprivation, the twice-daily forced head-first submersions in a barrel of iced water and, once, a savage, guard-organised gang rape, he fled via Hong Kong to Taipei, where helping hands succeeded in getting him to Europe. The New York exhibition, which I'd had to push hard and even call in certain long-owed favours to arrange, represented the first significant exposure of his art beyond the Chinese diaspora, and he chose that moment to unveil his masterpiece, a stunning coal and alabaster monstrosity that stood as both a personal catharsis and a towering defiance in the face of oppression, a roaring assurance that the human spirit can be beaten and brutalised but never broken, never completely silenced. Some who came looked and saw horror, others chose to recognise hope, but all understood, critics and public alike, that they were in the presence of a major piece of art.

In this way, between work and Alison, the bulk of my summer was taken up, and I confess that with my heart so violently dragged in such directions I had little time free to worry about Maggie. The night we'd spent around the Ouija board came to seem less and less real, until I could no longer easily connect with the emotions I'd felt in that peculiar darkness. And yet, a kind of dread did smoulder within me. I wrote and sent a letter in July, and followed it with a second in late August, short scribbled notes that were the only way I had of staying in touch. Both went unanswered, which deepened my sense of disquiet, but I tried not to let it bother me too much. Letters had fallen out of fashion. Few people sent them any more, and fewer still bothered to write in reply. And I understood artists, I knew what they were like when the work was flowing, when everything beyond the canvas became an inconvenience. But Maggie didn't need to write. A call would have sufficed, even a few words left on the answering machine, just to assure me that everything was as it should be. Because she didn't call, my concern began to eat up every spare minute.

And when I could bear no more, I laid out my diary, cancelled and rearranged a few things, and caught a flight to Cork. The relentless months of summer had worn me to a nub, both mentally and physically, but I'd worked hard and earned the time. My world could afford to stop turning for five days. The plan, only barely thought out, was to settle myself without fuss in Dublin and fall again into the embrace that I'd almost begun to believe had been imagined. West Cork would be a small detour, three-quarters of a day sacrificed in the best of causes. And worth it, Alison and I both agreed over the phone, for a little peace of mind.

★

Circumstances had changed since my previous visit. With September drawing to a close, the season's fringes were clearly evident. Late morning and early afternoon were warm and fine, with the sky a blue so pale as to be nearly colourless, but the implication of approaching winter felt undeniable. Probably because I knew the way, the road seemed to pass more quickly than before. I'd eaten at

The Dead House

Heathrow — coffee and two bacon sandwiches — and so decided to forgo the temptation of some Skibbereen nourishment, which allowed me to make decent time. Traffic was light, and practically non-existent once I'd crossed the Healy Pass, but as I neared the peninsula's western end and came to within touching distance of Allihies, the light seemed to shift, and the open sky closed in with a kind of shadowy whiteness. A pale thin hide of cloud raised itself in every direction, coating the day. I eased the hired car up onto the roadside verge just as the radio's three o'clock headlines were breaking yet more of their wearying sameness, and I listened for a moment then shut off the engine.

The silence came down hard. Without the glare of a summer sun, the land that lay spread out before me had become muted, and the ocean beyond was the flat, dry white of stone and less of a feature than I'd remembered. Even from this elevation and distance, though, the cottage remained imposing. The recent renovations had lost their buffed freshness and had begun to sport the first subtle bruises of time and weather, and the shadows seemed to fit the place better now than they had before.

Once again, I was struck by the absence of birds.

I followed the path down the hillside, thinking about how difficult it would be to hold your footing once the rains set in and the ground had turned to slush. Maggie had talked of plans to finish this path, but it was as I remembered, mud and cinders. I moved slowly, with gravity pressing like a hand against my back. Just ahead, the cottage loomed. I shuddered. All was calm, yet the overwhelming sense was that of tumbling headlong into something wrong. I knew I was being foolish but couldn't help myself.

As the ground levelled out I slowed my approach, searching the empty windows and straining to listen for the least evidence that I was not alone. But the world was still.

Ahead, the front door stood a few inches ajar. I eased it open a little further and called Maggie's name once and then again, the second time with more voice. There was no answer, and no sound at all apart from my own harried breathing. My urge was to turn away, to run. I had never wanted anything more. But instead, I stepped inside.

The air tasted foul. In the open doorway, cloying with a tinge of decay; worsening, once I'd advanced a few steps, to the rancid sweetness of meat gone bad and then far beyond. The living-room area, which I remembered as being so happily coloured, had become cluttered and dishevelled. Sheets of paper cloaked the walls, overlapping at careless angles and either smudged with charcoal or else laden and smeared in wide, senseless black and red brushstrokes. I was used to seeing Maggie's work in its rawest and most preliminary state, and had always assumed that I'd be prepared for anything where her art was concerned, even if and when she wandered beyond the Pale. Straining to absorb their detail in the poor light, I leaned in close and told myself that I could recognise elements of her style, a certain dextrous muscling of the brushwork, the vaguely familiar fall of the lines. But the truth was that these pictures – if that's what they even were – seemed to be something not only new but indefinable. Without sense or focus, devoid of subject matter, the paint lay in slobs across the paper, like the blistered welts of a recent flaying.

I turned away, not wanting to see any more, not wanting to have to think too much. But the turmoil was unceasing. Candle stubs in their dozens littered the table and fireside, and the old walnut and cherry tambour clock, inherited from her father's mother and which had been such a presence in all the homes of her life, now lay dead on the mantelpiece, stopped in vicious fashion by a nail driven through its face.

The other rooms were no better. The kitchen sink lay choked with weeks' worth of unwashed dishes, and the floor along its perimeters shifted with small things almost seen. Again my urge was to run, to get outside, away from the stench and the chill of anxiety, away even from this ground, which seemed to pulse with its own kind of horror. I had the feeling of being not only watched but studied. Mocked, even. The light inside was dim, as if something had been smeared into the glass of the windows so as to diffuse the daylight, and I felt constantly certain that I was about to be touched, grabbed. I was afraid. I admit it. Forget logic. The stillness and the sense of decay stirred a primal dread. Just wanting to get away, I hurried on. Her bedroom was a mess of torn and scattered books, tossed-aside items of clothing, crushed tubes of paint, the colours of some bloating like tongues from uncapped mouths, stained rags and wads of ruined paper, brushes poking their own odd angles from pint glasses and clear jars. Canvases large and mid-sized leant stacked three or four deep against the low of the walls, plastered in a relentless convolution of shapes, images that meant nothing to the eye but that somehow left a mark in you, a suggestion of something. The queen-sized bed lay tossed and dishevelled, the sheets pulled most of the way back to reveal in parts a heavily stained mattress, and a dark wool shawl masquerading as a curtain hung across the single narrow window, coming close to the sill on one side but drawing up short by several inches on the other. The day spilt in as an odd, boxy whiteness, but Maggie was not a part of it.

Outside, the air felt heavy, damp with heat and coming rain. I hurried beyond the reach of the cottage and then stopped and took several deep breaths. The taste of the house lingered, but the domineering flavour had become that of the ocean. I told myself that I could leave, that I'd earned the right. I'd looked and really looked. I'd done my duty, and that was enough. Except, it wasn't enough. I had to know. Too much had gone awry in the time since my last visit, some balance had been tipped. And Maggie was out here somewhere and clearly in need of help.

I surveyed the landscape. The world seemed deserted at first, the matted greenery, even after a hot summer, wild and overgrown, spilling down from the hillside towards the ocean with little but the occasional interruptions of rock to catch my eye. And then, down on the shoreline, something. A movement at first, a paleness indistinct against the stony water, but as I stared, and moved a few paces closer, it became recognisable as a figure, a girl or woman with long black hair, apparently naked, standing on the rocks and turned away from me, facing the ocean.

I almost called out. It didn't look like Maggie. A waif-like similarity, perhaps, but not quite her shape. Taller, I thought, and with the hair too dark and too long. But distance made me uncertain, and size was difficult to judge. So much had changed over these past months. I hurried down to the beach, cautious of the uneven ground, and the land rose and fell in ridges and clefts around me so that sometimes the figure was there, clearly a girl or young woman now, a stranger, and sometimes she was gone, hidden by the tuck of land. Confusion washed through me and quickened my pace still further until I was almost running, and then the pathway widened and I came to the beach a little out of breath, to find myself completely alone. The flint pebbles and cockleshells cracked and shifted beneath my last few steps and then there was no sound at all apart from the hush of the waves breaking hail-white across the strand.

Convinced that she must have gone in, that she had to have been stripped for swimming, I held my breath and waited, studying the surface, watching for the least break. But all I could see was the rise and spill of the waves, gentle but relentless, and after a minute or so, once it had become clear that nothing was coming up from that water, I went slowly towards the rocks that lay off to my left still wet and shining from the receding tide.

The sight of Maggie startled me. Tucked into a talon of sand beyond the first reef, she was kneeling before an easel and a mid-sized canvas, seemingly oblivious to everything but water and sky. When she heard her name being called, she turned, and what I saw then frightened me more than anything I'd so far seen. Still on her knees, her mouth moving to some silent chant, she'd become old, ruined. Her hair was a mess, spooling filthy and unkempt to her shoulders and in webs across her forehead, and her cheeks and eyes had sunken to pits in a way that fixed attention on the edges, the cheekbones, nose and chin. A simple paint-spattered grey cotton dress, sleeveless and thin as a nightgown, emphasised her emaciation, and I could see the spidery trace of her bones through the material's chalky, thinning skin. She watched, unmoved, as I clambered down from the rocks and seemed slow in recognising me. Even when I spoke her name, her trance held, a vagueness that kept her disconnected from the world and anchored instead to inner things.

'Maggie? Are you all right?'

'Hmm? Yes, fine. Thank you.'

Her voice was a blur of sound, the words shaping themselves in dazed fashion.

'I was up at the house. You haven't called in weeks. I was worried about you.'

She continued to gaze at me, and then something

shifted in her eyes and a kind of life returned to them. She smiled. I held her hands and helped her up from her knees, and standing in that spur of sand between the rocks we embraced for the longest time, with the intimacy of friends who held an unbreakable bond. Her hair and skin carried a putrid stench, the sharp vinegar reek of sweat and decay that in other circumstances would have caused me to draw back like I'd been burnt, but I felt such an overwhelming confusion of relief and dread that I couldn't even think of letting go. She'd always been slight, but now her breasts and hips pressed stony hard against me and the nubs of her spine raised themselves for the touch of my hand sliding the slow length of her back. In my arms, she felt as if she'd break under an extra pound of applied pressure, but I held tight anyway, not wanting to let go, not yet ready to give her up. I kissed her cheeks again and felt her smile, but finally, after what must have been close to a minute, and largely at her gentle prompting, we eased apart.

'You left your door open.'

'This isn't London, Mike. It's safe to do that out here.'

'Also, I think you might have mice.'

She shrugged. 'I hear them sometimes. At night, in the walls, coming down from the thatch. When they're not scratching, they make the sound of babies crying. And by day I only ever sense them ahead of me. They're like ghosts, or a bit like the wind. It's nice that they're nothing but movement.'

'Why don't we drive into Castletownbere? Get some traps. Maybe poison. And it'll give us a chance to catch up. If you like, I'll even let you buy me dinner.'

'No. I can't. Anyway, they're only mice. Just let them be. They don't bother anyone.'

Over her shoulder, I could see what she had been working on before I'd arrived. A skinned form of seascape, contorted from the surface facts and free of the late afternoon's pale, balmy comfort. Her ocean was a tartan of rust, loosely laid swathes of reds and tans, her huge clotted sky oppressive above the harried waves. Whether by accident or intent, she had achieved something I'd never thought possible: an almost complete diminution of technique, with all power derived completely from the subject matter. I wanted to say something, to ask her about it, to find the words that would express both my awe and my disquiet, but the painting seemed to demand silence. With effort, I averted my eyes.

The light thickened around us, the way it does after a late autumn day's sun has burnt itself out and left only its warmth behind, and I was surprised to find that it was already five o'clock. Without discussion, we gathered her belongings, she taking the canvas and leaving everything else, the easel, the box and scattered paint tubes, the jar of brushes, for me to carry. But it was only as we cleared the rocks and started back in the direction of the cottage that she seemed to properly register her surroundings, and the lateness of the hour. She stopped, gazed up along the beach and then, in a slow half-turn, out across the ocean, her eyes wide, her lips slightly apart. I stood, laden down with her belongings, and waited.

'Don't you think it's beautiful out here?' she said, as if seeing it all for the first time, or the first time in quite this way. I told her I did, and she turned, looked at me and settled into a smile that seemed touched with sadness. We walked on, without hurry, and I let her talk. She asked me about work, whether or not I was busy, if I was doing much travelling, if I'd made any decent sales, whether the market was currently bouncing or in a slump. And then the smile climbed back into place and she glanced at me and asked how Alison was keeping, these days, and if I'd slipped yet from my best behaviour. The softest possible breeze sifted the air, and for those few minutes, as we went, everything seemed almost fine again. She walked beside me, keeping to half an arm's length of distance, though probably not consciously so, and if I didn't look too closely it was just about possible to believe that she'd reverted once more to the Maggie I'd always known. Buoyant with the flavours of laughter, mischievous and full of inner serenity, and possessed of that stillness necessary for seeing everything as it needed to be seen. I was clinging to a false impression, of course, and I realised as much because distance gaped like a valley between us, but it didn't stop me from trying, and wanting, to believe.

'I paint every day,' she said, in answer to the question I hadn't asked. 'Something has changed for me. It's difficult to put into words. The isolation, I suspect. I breathe the work now, in a way I never did before. I feel like I'm being absorbed by the land. And I've begun to lose the concept of time. You know, this is a place that can't age. It changes faces sometimes, with the wind and the weather, but it always changes back. And the touchstones don't shift. It's about existing, as part of something bigger. Just look around and you'll get a sense of what I mean, but to really see it, to really feel and understand it, you have to look close. And that's what I'm doing now. I've started to see surfaces differently. Colours, too. As a child, did you ever stare at the world through a piece of coloured glass? Or plastic? Change the shades and everything changes. Try it for a while and you feel cut loose. You feel free. For me it's not that exactly, but it's like that. When I pick up a brush now, I'm no longer only painting scenes, I'm painting their insides, and their potential.'

I wanted to be happy for her. A tightness had come into her voice, a sort of pent-up ferocity that in another time and place, a classroom or studio, I'd have taken for passion. Here, though, in such isolation, it unnerved me, and it was all I could do to keep the distress out of my face. I smiled and nodded, told her that I had a waiting list of clients the length of both arms and as long again lined up for new work and that I'd be more than thrilled to take anything with me that she considered finished.

But she shook her head, no.

'The paintings themselves no longer matter. For a long time I couldn't understand that, but I get it now. When I finish something, it's lost to me. Sometimes I reuse the canvases, sometimes I need to burn them or throw them into the ocean. Give them to the tide. What counts is the work, the actual physical doing. That's the only art involved. The rest is just commerce. All these years, I never really knew what I was about, but these last few months the whole thing has become clear. I'm capturing moments. That's all. And once they're caught, something happens. They exist on canvas but they're dead. They're paintings, nothing more. Depictions. I do them and they're done.'

'But you need some income,' I said. 'You have to live, Maggie.'

The strand on our left side stretched eastwards as far as the eye could see, penned in and shaped into a curl by the sloping fields, and the water along its open side lay flat and seemingly still. Her gaze took her to the furthest point, where the last of the beach faded out of sight, and her voice, when it came, was a murmur, airy as sleep-talk.

'Every morning before the sun is up I climb the hills and sit in the druids' circle. I try to be there just as the day is getting light. I go even if it's raining, though I don't paint on those days, I just sit in the grass. I don't pray, but it's like praying. I suppose you could say, technically, that I'm trespassing, because it's farmland, and private property, but I've never seen anyone up there, and nobody has complained yet. Actually, it looks like the ground has been left to waste. But that's no surprise. Standing stones have a kind of magic about them. An energy. Around here, farmers won't interfere with such things. As I said, nothing really changes in a place like this.'

I could believe it. A lot of people are still ruled by superstition, especially in the country, where good and bad keep wider shades of grey. Nature runs through us like grain through wood, and it can be hard to break the habit of a thousand generations.

'The circle itself isn't particularly impressive,' she went on. 'Not like some you'll see. There are seven stones, one that comes to about my waist and the rest that reach maybe knee-high or a little bit less. The grass is long and lush, so the details aren't exactly distinct, a few have fallen over and look out of position, but when you think about how long they've been standing there it's nothing short of incredible, really, that there's any trace of them left at all. But there's a silence about the place that you'll find nowhere else. The air up there feels different. I don't know, alive, or something. As if the world is listening. On good mornings, when the sun starts to break the sky, you can see practically forever in three clear directions. And you sense the past in every breath. Two, three thousand years can slip away in a heartbeat. People talk all the time about haunted places, and that's certainly one. But I'm not sure it has much to do with ghosts, I think it just means it's held tightly by the past in ways that other places aren't.'

'And that's where you like to go to paint?'

'It's where I paint best. But I'd go there even if I never painted a line. It welcomes me in some way, opens me up.

Moves me. I must have finished twenty canvases up there, and taken hundreds of sketches. Sometimes I'll change angles, and the light is never twice the same. Those paintings are the most satisfying work I've ever done, because I can feel the place. Up there, the air runs through me. I've never been so connected to anywhere else. I don't know how else to explain it. Five years ago the paintings, and the sketches, would have made for a good exhibition. Maybe a great one.'

'Well,' I said, 'even if I can't sell them for you, will you at least let me see them?'

She shrugged. 'I can't. They're gone.'

'What? All of them?'

'It doesn't matter. I know them exactly. Down to the very stroke. They're gone, but they were gone the instant I finished painting them.'

'What did you do? Did you burn them?'

'Some I burnt. Others I cut up or painted over or threw off the cliffs. I like that best, because they float, and I can stand at a height and watch the tide carry them away. Though the fire is good, too. Satisfying. For the whispers and smell the paint gives off, and the colours of the smoke.'

I wanted to be angry rather than afraid, but both emotions seemed to spout from the same spring.

'Jesus, Maggie,' I said. 'You can't keep doing this. You'll run out of money soon, if you haven't already. From what I've seen, the house could certainly do with a bit more work. Those paintings could help you out, if you'd just let them.'

'I know. But I'm not ready to think about any of that. For now, I just want to paint. Nothing else matters, not money, not comfort. Nothing.'

'And this?' I indicated the canvas that she held outward at her side.

She glanced down. 'Part of my routine. I spend the mornings up at the stones. Afternoons and evenings I come down here and try to capture the ocean.'

I pretended then to scrutinise the picture, though by now I'd already studied it closely and could barely bring myself to even glance in its direction. Maggie, out of either habit or duty, raised it to chest height, the small slow trawl of her inhalations practically counting beats.

'It's stunning,' I said, doing what I could to sound truthful, and upbeat. It was stunning, too, but only in the fuller sense of the word. 'Visually, it takes your breath away, stops you cold. There's something, I don't know, a kind of menace. Something elemental. It makes me almost afraid. If I saw it on a wall in a gallery, I'd be hard pushed to recognise it as your style. I've never seen anything quite like it. If the rest of the stuff you've done is anything like this then your work seems to have taken a fairly dark turn.'

'This is how I see things now,' she said, with another shrug of her narrow shoulders, and her gaze fell away from me and fixed again on that distant point of beach. 'And this is how the world really is, if you want to know the truth. You should be afraid. We all should. Because none of us ever looks close enough to see. But once you peel back the surface, this is what lies waiting. This is all there is.'

★

We came up from the beach, following the same broken pathway as before. The uneven ground around us was sand and earth and mostly rock, combed with wiry sweeps of grass. Maggie, barefoot, seemed comfortable at my side, but then the cottage rose into view ahead and slightly to our right, and I felt an instant shift in her demeanour. She stopped, and turned to me.

'Well,' she said, in little above a whisper. 'Thanks for coming. There was no need, but thanks. It's good to know that someone cares. And I'll have some paintings to send on very soon. I promise. You can sell them if you want, or think about an exhibition. Or just give them away, if you feel like it. Whatever you want to do is fine. I'll leave it all to you.' She reached out and touched my arm just above the elbow. 'I owe you a lot, Mike. And I don't just mean money, either. I owe you everything.'

I shook my head, not yet ready to shoulder such responsibility. 'The only thing you owe me is a promise that you'll look after yourself, and that you'll make more of an effort to keep in touch. It's not good to cut yourself off so much from the world. A phone call, once in a while. That's all I ask. To me, or Alison. Or Liz, even. Just to let us know that you're still going strong.'

'I will. I promise. This is all my fault, dragging you out here for no good reason, making you worry over nothing. I shouldn't have let so much time go by. To be honest, I'm not sure where it went. But from now on I'll do better. I'll write, and call too, every chance I get. Once a week at least.'

From where we stood, we could see only part of the house's roof, the repointed chimney and the thatch dull as mud against the day.

'You can just leave the easel here, and the paints. I'll come back down for them. But it's getting late. You shouldn't be on these roads after dark. You can get a bed and breakfast in Castletownbere. The season for the tourists is finished so the guest houses will be quiet. Or you could make for Bantry, if you'd prefer somewhere with a bit more blood in its veins and don't mind the extra few miles.'

My mouth was dry and I could taste the ocean on every breath, in a way that was starting to make my throat hurt. For a few seconds, I wasn't sure how to respond.

'I was thinking,' I said, finally, 'that maybe I could just stay here tonight.'

'With me?'

'Well, just for tonight. If that's all right. To tell you the truth, I'm exhausted, and I really don't fancy the thought of more road. I've been working fifteen laps of the clock lately. And on top of that, I had the flight, and then the drive from Cork. Don't worry, I won't put you out. And I'll leave early. I have an engagement in Dublin. An armchair will do just fine. All I want is to get my head down and sleep. Even if only for a few hours.'

'I'm afraid I'm not set up for visitors. There's nothing in, I haven't been to the shops.'

'That's all right. No problem. I can pop in to Allihies. Grab a few things. Fish and chips, something like that. Even cold food is fine. Bread, cheese. Whatever you fancy.'

In three-quarter profile, she seemed on the brink of tears.

Something odd happened to the moment then, as if a flash of past was brought into overlap, attaining a kind of duality. I saw that the beauty was gone from her face but also that it was all around her, present but separate, like a veil. In that instant, the person she'd been measured itself against the person she had become. Then, as I watched, the skin at the corners of her eyes pinched with what I can only believe was fear. Slowly, sadly, she shook her head.

'You can't stay, Mike. I'm sorry. I have to be alone. He doesn't like outsiders in the house.'

'Who doesn't?'

'The Master.'

The shaping of the word, even in her own hushed voice, struck her with the ferocity of a slap. She turned away, and her eyes, wide and glassy, again found and held to the roof of the cottage above the scrub. Instinctively, I looked in that direction too, but whatever she saw eluded me. Instead, a sense memory flamed awake, the festering, rotten-meat stench that I'd earlier experienced. But there was nothing out of place, nothing to bother the stillness. The low hush of the early evening tide continued to carry over us from behind and even as we stood there, close enough to touch but not touching, the light gave up its shadowy glow and the edges of the world around us were gently lost, blurred by the smothering dusk. And I felt sick to my stomach.

'I'll write,' she whispered. 'And I'll call. I promise. Now go. Please.'

I just stared at her. 'What are you saying?'

'He knows you. He remembers. And he doesn't want you here. You have to leave.'

'Maggie, this is insane talk. That night was just a game, a bit of fun. Nothing happened.'

'Please, Mike. If you have any feelings for me at all. And I know you do. I'm asking you to go. There's nothing to worry about. Everything is fine. I'll call you tomorrow at Alison's.'

I should have refused to leave, or at least refused to leave without her. I had every logical excuse on my side: how far she'd let herself go, the sheer squalor of her living conditions and, most significantly, her obvious psychological deterioration. Even apart from the candid reference to a supernatural entity, one that seemed to have gained dominion over her increasingly contracting world, her artwork was clearly the product of a delusional mind. In hindsight, I know what I should have done. I had a duty to resist, and to save her, even if only from herself. But the truth, to my great shame, is that I was frightened.

I told myself that my fear was for her. She'd always

tended towards fragility, and the years of physical and mental abuse, followed by such sudden and complete isolation, was a weight too great to bear. The assault that put her in hospital had been brutal and depraved, unimaginable, really, in its magnitude, but even after the scars and broken bones began to heal, the memories kept her on a brink. And either by accident or with intent, she'd used her time alone to dredge the most repressed and isolated corners of her mind, until the cracks and fissures opened into chasms.

But there was something else. The house, and this place, had played a part. In a city, with its crowds and traffic noise, reality is a sheet of thick glass, solid and impenetrable. But out here, it is a far less certain state. Out here, just like the ocean, it pulls to tide and current. And, just like the ocean, its surface can be easily broken.

Such casual mention of something supernatural disturbed me, but at its base level my anxiety was a selfish one, fuelled with dread that whatever was happening to Maggie could somehow happen to me. Something about this landscape, beautiful as it was, inspiring as it must have been with its rare light and aura of ancient magic, troubled me at an almost primal level. Solitude could be treacherous to certain minds, and while I was stronger, and probably far less sensitive, far less attuned to these vibrations, that did not mean I couldn't be broken down.

I made an excuse. I told myself that by gatecrashing her situation I'd very likely threaten the precarious balance of her mind, maybe even pitch her into some kind of irreversible psychosis. She had survived until now, not unscathed but at least retaining a basic level of functionality, and even though the evidence of her suffering was irrefutable she'd obviously found or developed some sort of coping mechanism and would surely continue to get by until I could return with the proper help.

'All right,' I said, giving in. 'I'll go.'

I set down the easel and the box of paint, came close and drew her once again into my arms. She allowed this but did not bodily respond. Her arms hung to her sides, and her frame lay slight and limp against me, alive only with the slow, gentle pull and ease of her breathing. I held her for as long as I could, not really wanting to let go but more than a little hurt, too, at her lack of reciprocation or even response, then finally kissed her cheek and took a step back.

The way she was then, during those following seconds, is how I continue to picture her now, in my mind. Bedraggled, ruined, her narrow shoulders hunched with a kind of inherent grief, her naked arms thin as cane, her scant cotton dress filthy from days or even weeks of wear, her small feet naked and pale against the dirt, her huge wide eyes the same pond-green that I'd always known, a bottomless shade, but shining now, glassy with some kind of imbued semi-trance. I had seen her in beauty, on her best days, of which there had been many, but the way she was then, in that moment, is the recollection that dominates, maybe because of the guilt I feel, the knowledge that through my casual abandonment I'd helped cause or at least enabled such degeneration.

Not knowing what else to say or do, I turned and started on ahead, careful without thinking about it to skirt the cottage in a wide sweep. As before, the incline that led up to the road pulled at my breathing, and when I at last looked back she was still standing exactly where I'd left her, in the lowing half-light. I raised a hand in goodbye, but she did not wave back. And in the distance, a hundred or so yards further on against the now dark ocean, I again made out what I took to be that figure of the girl or woman, standing on the reefs. The same as before, dark-haired and naked, her body a pale, stubborn filament against the darker shades of rock and water. As I watched, she appeared to turn away from the ocean, sensing, it almost seemed, that she was no longer quite alone. From such distance, it was impossible to tell where her gaze settled, but a coldness flushed through me. I got into the hired car and started the engine. I had already seen too much.

★

Dublin kept its own season, the lurid lamplit streets slashed by gales and the low-slung sky a murky, tallow dark, thick with the suggestion of more and worse to come. The sensible course of action would have been to get a room in either Castletownbere or Bantry, in keeping with Maggie's advice, but both felt too close to Allihies. I knew that if I were to stop for the night, I'd be unable to resist the urge once morning broke to go back out there, and I think I was afraid of what I might find waiting. So, instead, I pushed on, even though I was in no fit state to drive, and because the roads proved relatively quiet for a Wednesday, I made Cork city a little before eight and Dublin somewhere around half ten. I arrived, unannounced but not unexpected, weary and fractured from the long road, and glad to my soul that I'd forced these five days open in my schedule.

That night I refused to think about anything beyond the immediate. I was alive, and it was all right to let myself be happy within the moment. Alison and I ate something sweet and sour from a Chinese takeaway and by accident got through a couple of bottles of a better than decent Chilean Malbec, and I remember that there was a flash of pure insight somewhere in the mix, watching her walk barefoot into the kitchen for the second bottle, when everything about us and about myself slammed into place. She'd hesitated in the doorway and glanced back over one shoulder, and when she saw me watching she smiled in such an open manner that I knew, suddenly and without doubt, there was love involved, and that this was exactly what I wanted from my life. The rest was just clutter. Only this was real.

We sat together for a long time, a couple of hours at least, side by side on the couch, our arms and shoulders touching, our talk flowing as freely as the wine. The song of her voice was irresistible, a soft vibration of sound that made its way inside me and lit a fire, and I told her as much, which at once embarrassed her and made her happy. We didn't really need the alcohol but it helped soften the edges, and made it easier to sidestep the subject of my detour to Cork. Alison didn't push, knowing I'd open up to her when I was ready, but that I was a while yet from such a conversation and too raw to face up to what had happened down there.

The Dead House

Instead, we spoke of other things, everything and nothing, the words themselves far less important than our inter-action. Work, of course, new artists I'd seen or heard of, the sales she'd made in recent weeks, and about the world in general, the joys and headaches of living in Dublin and London, my recent business in New York, places we'd been in our respective lives and places we'd love, for a variety of reasons, to see or see again. For her, Cuba, Sicily, Egypt; for me, the Marquesas, French Polynesia, the runaway world of Gauguin and Brando and Robert Louis Stevenson. The words were just a balm, floating dreams, but a way of reconnecting. And then, draining what must have been her third or fourth glass, she leaned in, kissed me and said in a deep sigh how good it felt, us being together like this. How right. I drew her against me and left unmentioned the depth and breadth of my surprise at just how much I'd missed her during our time apart, how many times a day she entered my mind and how, when my phone rang at night, my heart upped its rhythm, knowing it would be her.

★

The Dead House

The following morning, I woke alone from a deep, consuming sleep. I'd slept past seven o'clock for the first time in months, maybe in years, and for a minute or so, before the world fell in on me again with all its shapes and edges, I lay very still in that big strange bed, confused and disoriented. The room's décor was comfortably spare, the blanched colour choices emphasised by a burden of smudged light that filtered in through the tall rain-scudded casement window. Beyond the glass, the Dublin sky moiled. And then, like photographic paper slowly giving up its captured truth to the plunge of a chemical bath, memories of the night before began to break the surface, and with them, a yawning calm. Naked beneath the heavy duvet, I kept my breathing to sips, afraid that I might somehow dispel the idyll.

Beyond the open doorway a radio was playing, low music that I recognised but couldn't quite identify, and from the kitchen the kiss and splatter of bacon in a pan. I listened for Alison, but her movements, if she was even there, were silent. I thought of calling out, hoping that I could perhaps lure her back to bed, but instead I pushed away the bedclothes, got up and slowly dressed while watching the traffic build in murmurs on the North Circular Road. Already, the day felt caged, the sky laden with the kind of dirty heft that tightened every expression, even smiles, a half-turn beyond comfort.

'You're up,' she said, when I entered the kitchen.

I nodded, crossed the room to where she was standing with a wooden spatula, kissed her mouth and then took a seat at the table. She'd made a pot of tea, and I started to pour but stopped because it was still too weak, and instead leaned back in my chair to watch her. She had her hair up in a loose mess, exposing the glassy nape of her neck, and wore a bulky pale blue flannel dressing gown, a couple of sizes at least too big, fastened by a matching belt snugly double-knotted across the waist. I watched her break eggs into the pan and smiled to myself at the slightly childlike way she had the cuffs of her sleeves turned up, exposing so many inches of wrist, obviously in an effort to keep her hands free from obstruction. And then the thought broke in my mind that the gown, given its size, must have belonged to someone else, and I turned my head away so as not to have to see too much of her history. People have pasts, of course, the grain of which runs often to the bone, and sometimes it can be difficult to let all the way go. I didn't blame her or hold the facts of her life against her, but this particular morning I simply wanted to spare myself such details.

'Did you sleep well?'

'I did. A lot better than I expected to. You?'

She turned her head and offered a quick profile grin in reply. I nodded again, to myself this time, and once more chanced pouring the tea.

'The wine, I expect. That always puts me out cold.'

'I don't know,' I said. 'I'm not sure I'd give so much credit to the wine.'

On the radio a peculiar, asexual voice seemed to be discussing rather than announcing the weather forecast, its continually questioning pitch caging it into a one-sided conversation. The accent wavered, an affected mid-Atlantic twang less than successfully cloaking the occasional but elongated jabs of throaty mountain Irish. But it didn't matter; the important words on offer were wind and rain, variations thereof. I waited for music and tried not to feel too disappointed when it arrived, it being the sort of pop that they continually peddle as classic these days but which, by my reckoning, lands about twenty-five years too late for that status.

After a few minutes, Alison brought me a plate piled with three strips of bacon, two sausages, mushrooms, tomato and two softly fried over-easy eggs, exactly how I like them, and she sat down and began buttering enough toast for

both of us. That amused me, though I didn't let it show. I
took a slice from her, tore a piece free and used it to break
open one of my eggs. She sipped tea, and there was a light-
ness in her face, a happiness I think, that made me blush a
little, though I am not usually the blushing kind.

'Fried eggs need to be eaten hot,' I said, the only thing I
could think of to say.

We ate without much talk. I tend towards small breakfasts – a bowl of muesli, or porridge if I'm not in too much
of a hurry – and fried breakfasts like this are a genuine
treat, something I never make for myself and which I tend
to eat only when I am away from home, staying in some
hotel. But this morning I was ravenous, and the sausages, in
particular, were like nothing I'd ever tasted before: a pork
and apple variety, she told me, when I asked, a speciality of
one of the butchers in town.

'So tell me about Maggie,' she said, after letting me finish.
She poured us both a second mug of tea. 'How bad is it?'

'It's not ... I'm not sure that "bad" is exactly the right
word. Because how would you define bad? And you know
what she's like, how she gets. The paintings, I don't know.
She gives them too much of herself.'

'But you're worried.'

'Worried? No. Not really. I wouldn't say worried.'

'I would. You drove a couple of hundred miles out of your way yesterday. If everything was fine you'd have said something last night. But you didn't. And I could feel how tense you were.'

'That wasn't all tension.'

'Come on, Mike. Be serious.'

'Well, all right, maybe I am a little worried. But there's good reason, I think. It's that place. Christ. How can anyone live out there? And she's really let it go. And herself, too. I have a tendency sometimes to overreact, and I keep wondering if it's maybe not as bad as I think. But it is. You should see it. And you know what's gone on with her, that she's had her problems.'

'That's putting it mildly. A problem is when the toilet gets backed up or when the neighbour starts blaring heavy metal at three in the morning. What she went through was streets beyond any of that.'

'Right. Which is why it can't be such a good idea for her to be so isolated. I've always thought that, right from the beginning, and I know it for certain now. But there's no talking to her.'

Alison held her mug tented between the fingertips of both hands, and took the tea in a series of rapid sips. I saw that on her left wrist was the delicate gold chain that

I'd bought for her in Edinburgh. It fell against her skin in easy fashion, in a way that seemed comfortable. She wore no other jewellery, no nail varnish either. Her hands were clean and pale, with a certain small-animal fragility.

'Well,' she said, over the brim of her mug. 'Is she working, at least?'

'She's doing nothing else.'

'Really? But that's good, isn't it?'

'I don't know. It should be, of course, but I'm really not sure. From what I've seen, the whole thing has gone beyond obsessional. I think she might be in the middle of some kind of breakdown. You should see her, Ali. She's in ruins. It's like she has no control over herself. Christ, it's almost, I hate to say it because I know how it'll sound, but it's almost as if she's possessed. The whole time I was there she seemed like someone hypnotised. Her hair is a mess, she's lost so much weight that her bones are showing white through her skin, and I don't think she's washed herself in weeks. Nobody gets like that by choice. And the new stuff, the paintings. God.'

'You've seen them?'

'Not exactly, not to study. Glimpses, mostly. When I searched the house, I found a few leaning against a wall in the bedroom, but the room was murky and it was hard

to take in the detail. Actually, the main thing on my mind,
if you want to know the truth, was getting out of there.
The place had such a bad feeling about it. The only painting I had a chance to properly consider was the latest, the
one she'd been working at down on the beach. A work in
progress. I don't know, maybe it's me who's losing it. Artists
have a process, don't they? And there are no rules to say
it can't change over time. Maybe this is how she needs to
work now. Her head must be wrecked from all she's been
through. It's difficult to know what to think. But I can't
help feeling there's something wrong. Something outside
herself. I know, I realise how it sounds. Talking like this, I
sound mad even to myself. But most of what she paints,
she destroys. That's if she's to be believed. And that's not
normal. She's always had a tendency towards such behaviour, but in the past it's been about the chase for perfec-
tion, about trying to make the work fit the vision. And
she could always be made to listen, and to see sense. But
this is different. What she's working on now, even from the
little I've seen, isn't like anything else she's ever done. Not
her style at all. I know her work better than anyone in the
world, just about, I could pick out one of her pieces from
a pile of a thousand expert forgeries. It has to do with the
weight of her hand on the canvas, and the way she pulls the

brush. Maybe in watching her develop and evolve over so many years I caught something of the feel of the work. So I've always been able to understand her changes in direction, even when some of the turns taken were fairly wild. But if you put this new stuff in front of me I'd never be able to ascribe it to her. That's how much she's changed. Certain elements can be recognised if you look closely, but they're largely suggested.'

'And you're sure you're not exaggerating?'

'Do you think I am?' I shrugged. 'Maybe. I'm not sure of anything any more. At least not where Maggie is concerned. How can I be? But what I do know is that the cottage has been let fall apart. She had the place so nice, too. Remember? But you'd hardly recognise it now. It's filthy, the mice are back, nesting in the thatch, the walls are decked with sheets of paper smeared in paint and charcoal, and there's a stench like you wouldn't believe. The smell of dead things. I don't generally put a lot of stock in what passes for normal, but I just can't accept that anybody should be living like that, and I certainly don't buy that anyone would live that way by choice. Tell me if it sounds like I'm overreacting because I'll be more than glad to rein myself in, but that's how I feel.'

Alison rose from the table and set to boiling water for

more tea. She said nothing, just stood there, gazing out of the window at, I suppose, the road and footpath below, the lapels of her dressing gown bunched in one tight fist just beneath her throat. I waited, trying not to watch, but her movements between the kettle and the sink kept grabbing at me. A song came on the radio, something vapid, a girl's voice slurring words only just saved from being empty as space by an annoying but catchy melody playing out over the same generic drum and bass slam that seems all you need now to make an impact in the charts. Well, that and a willingness to show off nine and a half tenths of your ass and then act outraged when someone brands you a slut or a prostitute.

'I called Liz a month or so back,' she said. 'You remember Liz.'

'The poet? Yeah, of course.'

'She and I have kept in touch. We got on really well that weekend and often call one another up, just to chat. Did I tell you I've started carrying her books in my gallery? A small display of signed copies beside the reception desk. No commission or anything, it's just to help her out, and to bring something a bit different to the place. They're selling, too, especially to the tourists. Anyway, she lives in Bantry, as you know.'

'I remember her talking about the mythology of the place.'

The kettle came to the boil and switched itself off. Alison scalded the pot, dropped in three teabags and added the water.

'She told me that she'd stopped in a few times to see Maggie. Not as often as she should have, she said, but who can blame her for that? Life gets in the way. It happens to the best of us. But over the course of a summer, three or four visits isn't bad. Her first call was just a couple of weeks after we'd all been there. They spent a nice hour or so eating a lunch of some cold meats and deli salads that she'd brought with her, and chatting and laughing about the likelihood or otherwise of either one of them snagging a local farmer. One of the heavyset, ruddy-faced types that you'd see in the post office or supermarket in Allihies, she said, men who cut their own hair and chew incessantly on a bit of cheek, and who move through the aisles and along the road as if they can still feel the saddle beneath them. Light-hearted conversation, perfect for a summer's afternoon. But when she made it out that way again, maybe three weeks later, something had changed. Small differences, she said. Cups and plates piled abandoned in the sink, the clean edge taken off the living room. Maggie herself seemed fine, if a little distracted. Her eyes kept slipping into stares and her voice had fallen to a murmur. As if the air had gotten in. She mentioned that she'd been spending a lot of time outside, that she'd started sketching again and was thinking about breaking out the brushes. Liz recognised the sensation of vagueness, because she herself got that way sometimes when a poem really took hold of her. But with Maggie it seemed magnified, and she wondered if perhaps there might have been something else involved. A smoke, pills, something that dulled the facts just enough.'

I thought about it as I poured the fresh tea. Drugs. On one level it made sense, and yet it didn't quite cover all the bases. In some ways, the idea probably raised more questions than it answered.

'A mental problem might be a better fit,' I said. 'Bipolar, maybe, or schizophrenia. They say that the least thing can set people off. Her hospital stint could have provided the trigger. Or the solitude she'd found. After London, so much quiet had to be a massive shock to the system.'

The colour seemed to seep from Alison's face. She put down her mug and stared at me.

'Ali? What's the matter?'

'Liz mentioned something else, too,' she said, in a voice almost too small to hear. I had to lean in to catch the words. 'They were standing in the doorway, and just as she was turning to leave she heard something. A noise from the bedroom, as if there was somebody else in the house, the lumbering sound of something heavy being dragged or dragging itself across the floor. She was startled, but Maggie's demeanour didn't shift. "It's just the Master," she said, her voice as calm as the afternoon, and with a smile of goodbye she stepped back inside and shut the door.'

'Jesus. Why didn't you tell me this before?'

'I don't know. I suppose I didn't want to make anything of it. That night with the Ouija board really frightened me. It was such a stupid idea. You'll probably think I'm acting like a child but for the better part of a week after, the only way I could get to sleep was by leaving the light on in the en-suite. I had to prop the door open. But even with the light, I suffered the most horrific nightmares. Unrepeatable stuff. A couple of nights, I actually borrowed a friend's dog, a hyperactive little Bichon Frise named Tufty, and had him sleep in the room with me just so I wouldn't have to be on my own.

'Something came through to us that night, Mike. Nothing will convince me otherwise. And it was as if it had in some way attached itself to me. I was being foolish, of course, but I couldn't free myself of the notion. What matters is that it felt real. God, I get chills just thinking about it. And I don't even want to imagine what it must be like for Maggie, having to sleep in that cottage without the security of companionship. Say what you want about Dublin, or London, or any city. Any town, even. If you scream, somebody will surely hear. They mightn't exactly come running, but they'll hear. I'd die and turn to dust if I had to be Maggie for a night, if I had to spend a night alone in that house.'

'A night? Based on what I saw yesterday, the condition of the place and the feeling of it, even an hour would be too long. Even in broad daylight.'

'It got so bad that, finally, I spoke on the phone with Liz about it. I just couldn't get away from the memories. And you know how it is when you can't sleep. What it does to you. New details would come to the surface every time I closed my eyes or had a spare minute to think. I implored of her to admit that it was all just a prank, that she'd been manipulating the glass the whole time and had put Maggie up to playing along. I even cried. That's how deeply I was affected by it all. But she swore to me that she'd done nothing. And I believed her. I didn't want to, but the heart decides these things. You can list all the evidence you want but there's no way you can make yourself believe something, just like you can't make yourself not believe. I know what I saw, and what I felt. I wish it were different, but that's it. And Liz felt much the same.

'Over the few days that followed, we talked a lot. It was good to have somebody to bat these thoughts around with, someone who understood the need. I could have talked to you, I know, but the truth is that I'd have felt ridiculous. I suppose I didn't want to compromise what we had going. And I didn't want you seeing me as some kind of a flake. Because men view things differently, don't they? I'm not saying all men, but generally speaking. There's an inbuilt pragmatism. With Liz it was easy to talk, I think because neither one of us cared much about looking foolish in front of the other, but also because, essentially, we were both chasing some kind of explanation, at least at first. Anything, however far-fetched, that would allow us keep a semblance of logic. We ran through the various possibilities. A prank, somebody's teasing taken a bit too far, a cable running under the floor that might explain away the vibration in the glass, some kind of mass hallucination brought on by the combination of alcohol, circumstance and the inevitable supernatural associations with a Ouija board. All seemed vaguely plausible, but none felt right, and finally, realising there were no easy answers to be found, we instead set about trying between us to recall the exact wording of the messages that had come through. And we uncovered something.'

'The one in Irish.'

She paused, studied me openly. 'That's right. *An bhfuil cead agam teacht isteach.* Liz was terribly worried about it. She'd written it out on the night and held on to the notepad. And it seems that her translation skills were just the tiniest bit off. She'd read it initially as the spirit or whatever it was, the Master, asking for permission to join us, which of course we all accepted as part of the game and even, to our shame, on some level probably welcomed. My own recollection of Irish is limited to about fifteen words, so there was little I could offer in the way of assistance, but I've looked it up since and her interpretation was reasonable enough, given the circumstances. Unfortunately, though, it does seem that, if taken in a larger sense, the words can also be seen to suggest something slightly different. A more accurate translation of the phrase might be, "Can I enter?"'

A shudder ran through me. Just for a second, I was back in the cottage, around the table, watching Maggie's face yellowed and shifting in the candlelight.

'Subtle differences are still differences,' Alison went

on. 'Even on the phone, I could tell that Liz was upset. And worried, too. It was in her silences. A kind of weight. Because the new words seemed so full of implication. That same day, she got in the car and drove out there, and she tried visiting a couple of times more, but on each occasion found the house empty. The first time, she only went to the door of the cottage, but after that she searched the surrounding area, even went down onto the beach and called out. But she received no answer.'

Outside, it had begun to rain. It came in scuds against the glass and gave the light a wearying heft that made me want to finish or abandon the tea and return to the warmth and safety of bed. On the radio, news again broke through the music, the same genderless voice as before spouting the same words I'd already heard: political white noise, bank debt, a suicide bomber somewhere far away, an earthquake in one of the northern Indian cities, measuring seven and a half on the Richter scale, the damage already estimated in the low to mid hundreds of millions. I listened anyway, out of some misplaced duty, and wondered when exactly we'd started counting casualties in dollar terms rather than in the number of dead and injured. The grease from my breakfast had begun to congeal, coating the flat of the plate with a waxy skin. When I looked up, Alison was watching

me, her chin resting on one fist. I wanted to reach out for
her and hold on tight.

'What are you thinking?'

I shrugged. 'What's there to think?'

'That we should drive down.'

'What? No. We only have a few days, Ali. I can think of
better ways to spend the time.'

'Come on. I know you don't mean that. And it'll be different with two of us. It'll give you an easy mind, having
two perspectives instead of one. It'll help you to make sense
of things. You're troubled. Deny that all you want but I can
see it. And Maggie is our friend.'

'I'm overreacting, that's all.'

'Well, so what? Even if you are, it'll be a day out for us.
A nice drive. And we'll be together.'

For a few seconds I said nothing. Then I sighed.

'It's just that she's fragile, you know? And she has always
been so blind in chasing happiness. The last boyfriend,
Pete, was some piece of work. One of those tailored types,
everything designer. Supposed to be some kind of a financial whizz-kid, probably up to his tonsils in this current
mess. Probably a good percentage of the cause, I'd say. It
wouldn't at all surprise me. But Maggie thought the sun set
with him. When I found out he'd put her in the hospital

I slipped a crowbar under the front seat of my car, just in case I happened to get lucky. Looking back, maybe it was a good thing that I didn't find him. In my entire life I never committed even a single act of violence, but there were a few days around that time when I think I might have been capable of something terrible. Christ, Ali, you should have seen her. The swelling turned her eyes to slits. He'd kicked and punched her, took out teeth, broke her arm, ribs. Assaulted her sexually, too. One of the nurses told me, in confidence. They knew from the bruising. A depraved attack, was how the nurse described it. She'd spoken in a whisper, said it was among the worst she'd ever seen. The nurse spared me the details but the horror of it had numbed her expression. Maggie and I never discussed it, and I never let on that I knew, but she wasn't stupid. She was passing blood and for a while they were extremely worried about her kidneys. If I hadn't known it was her in the bed the first time I walked in, if the nurses hadn't assured me, I don't think I'd have even recognised her. That's how bad she looked, how beaten. And she just lay there, calm and still, accepting of it all, as if she deserved no better. I can still see the marks of his thumbs on her throat, red welts from where he'd tried to strangle her. So, yeah, I suppose I am worried for her. I always worry, because she's just so incapable of recognising danger. Even if there's nothing wrong with that house and that place, I don't think she's safe. The isolation might be good for her art, and the land-scape is so wide open and so wild it probably does inspire her and give her the time and space and freedom that she needs to work, to explore her depths or whatever it is that artists do. But cutting herself off from the world can't be healthy. I know her. If we're not careful, if we don't do what we can to help, she'll break beyond the point of repair.'

★

The drive down to Cork acted as a balm. The outer world barely penetrated, apart from the radio, which we kept tuned to an oldies station and turned low except when something decent came on – Creedence, Bob Seger, Neil Young, maybe something by the Stones – and then either Ali or I would crank it up a click or two beyond comfort level and we'd sing along to the parts we half-remembered, making a mess of everything but loving it, loving being together, laughing our way through. Our reason for being on the road didn't fade but felt as if it could, for a while, anyway, be put aside. I kept glancing at her, wanting to see the hidden parts of who she was, and to be able to decipher the happy thoughts that fish-hooked the nearest corner of her mouth towards a smile. Sometimes she'd reach up to tuck a strand of hair that had worked its way loose back behind her ear, but mostly she sat with her hands folded in her lap, fingers loosely entwined, her jawline tightening whenever I spoke, a barely perceptible gesture that accompanied her absolute attention.

By Urlingford a smothering mist had descended, one that significantly hindered visibility but lent something quite pleasant to the late morning. I kept well inside the speed limit and there was no further discussion as to what might lie ahead. We no longer needed those words, now that we had committed ourselves to this. Instead, we talked mostly of our own situation, slow-dancing, careful with our steps. When I needed to be back home, what the rest of my year looked like, how we could best work the gaps in our respective calendars. The fact that she could be in London in little more than an hour, or that I could get to Dublin, seemed to stoke our optimism. I knew that I'd have a few days at the beginning of November, if she could arrange for cover at the gallery, but there was also the very slim possibility of a weekend somewhere in between. And outside, beyond the rain-dappled glass, the wind fell away. The towns we passed through took on a drab, spectral stillness, and the fields, paled by the swollen mists, softened beyond any depth or definition.

For sustenance, we stopped at a small place in Cashel, a café with bohemian delusions, the décor keeping to bright yellows and hearty pinks, ordered a first and then second cup of good coffee to wash down the ham, cheese and chutney submarine sandwiches. It was a pleasant and necessary diversion, the chance to sit and relax and for fifteen or twenty minutes act like normal, happy, well-adjusted human beings. We ate, staring out at the drizzling street and imagining aloud how it might be to live here, in a town like this, and never know anywhere else, the way people of certain generations did, or must have. Ali suggested that some could be content with such a life, while others would only ever feel imprisoned, that it depended on the individual heart. But for us, the road kept calling.

Allihies lay some three hours further on. The mist thickened as we neared the coast, a veil heavy enough to obliterate the landscape and reduce the mountains to smoke and shadow. When I brought the car to a stop, there was total silence. The world was still. We sat there, hot and tired, mentally bracing ourselves for what might come, until a smell of burn began to permeate the freshened air. For a second or two my mind flashed with a panicked thought for the engine, but this was different, less immediate, the greenish stench of charred timber.

Alison unclasped her seat belt. 'Something's on fire.'

I shook my head. 'No,' I said. 'Something was.'

We got out and hurried down the hillside, holding hands to keep from falling and with our free hands pressed to our mouths. The air around us had the soft white look of spun sugar, all false, clotted purity, its illusion ruined by every taken breath. Then the blackened trace of the cottage pressed into view. I stopped, causing Alison to step against me. Her breath laboured dryly against my neck, and I caught some of her unease to multiply with my own and tightened my grip on her hand.

'Christ, Mike,' she whispered, as if afraid of being overheard. 'What happened here?'

Her words, coming from so close and hard as they were, caused an itch deep inside my ear. The charred stench felt complete in its invasion, its stinging sharpness realigning the shape of her face, and almost certainly my own, into a domineering rictus. And because there was no wind at all, you could hear the waves breaking soft hushes against the beach away in the distance off to our right.

'Do you think she got out?'

It was the question I had not allowed myself to consider.

I wanted to say yes, of course, but when I tried to speak no words came. The roof of the cottage was gone, the thatch burnt to grit, the beams collapsed inward. Beside me, Alison began, very softly, to cry. I put my arm around her shoulders, kissed her cheek, which even during those few seconds had already become coated in a skin of ash, and held her. But only for a moment. Because I had to know.

Instead of entering directly, I circled the premises. The devastation was immense. The roof had mostly fallen in and the chimney collapsed. The glass had exploded from the windows, ash coated the walls, and the back door was gone. I leaned against the jamb and called Maggie's name, but my voice, too full of scrapings, didn't feel like mine, and the sound lingered for longer than was right in the bitter air. The heat's immensity, which must have reached the levels of a furnace, had broken things down at a chemical level. The result was evisceration. I called out again, and again the name hung there, the sound of it hopeful, almost curious, and then detached, free of all feeling, all emotion, and then, finally, forlorn. When it passed, I put my handkerchief to my mouth, started inside and, with caution, aware that the walls could at any moment come in on me, began to work my way through the rooms. But there was little to see. In the kitchen, living room and bedroom, everything had been taken by the flames: all the furniture, her clothes, her paintings. The damage was so complete that I had trouble remembering it as it had been. Shards of crockery crunched beneath my feet, and the few remaining roof beams groaned like old sailing ships resigning themselves to a windless drift. Though the fire had clearly burned itself out several hours earlier, its heat held to the more confined spaces, a cloying, suffocating reek of sulphur. Only the second bedroom, the smaller of the two, which Maggie had never properly gotten around to decorating, had been spared the worst of the blaze, and in there, incredibly, a few canvases survived intact, propped face-inward against the side of a child's pale oak chair. Three were of medium size and two were slightly smaller, maybe twelve inches by eighteen, and I gathered them up and hurried outside, carrying them at angles across my chest.

Alison stood waiting, twenty feet or so back from the house. We didn't see one another until I'd come very close, and the flattened grass must have muffled my footsteps because I startled her into a small scream, even though she'd been expecting me with every breath. I put the canvases down, and she hurried to me and held me. The stench of the fire clung to my body and hair, and I felt as if I'd taste of it forever, that no matter how much I washed I'd never be free of it again. After a moment, she took the handkerchief from my clenched fist, found the cleanest corner and began to wipe the grime from my eyes, nose and mouth. I stood there and let her, gasping and waiting for my head to clear. I was sweating heavily and had begun to feel very cold.

'Is she—'

I shook my head, no.

'You're sure?'

'She's not in there, Ali.'

She started to say something else, stopped, and went again, 'Is there any chance that she's been—'

'There'd be traces. The fire was hot, but it wouldn't have melted bone. She must have gotten out.'

'Maybe some of the people from the village came. If they'd seen the smoke or smelled the flames, they'd have had to, wouldn't they? Maybe they dragged her out.'

'It's possible. But it looks as if it probably burned through the night. And we're quite cut off out here. I'm not sure that anyone would have noticed. The smoke mightn't have been visible from Allihies. More likely, she got out, probably before it really started to go, and is still around here somewhere.'

'What do you want to do?'

The Dead House

I sighed. 'What I want to do is go back to Dublin with you and lie in a bath for a couple of hours. Try to get some of this smoke off me and soak myself back to some state of normality. But what I need to do, what we need to do, is find her. If her mind really isn't right, anything could happen. And in this fog, it won't be safe for her to be wandering about.'

'Good, then let's stop standing here.'

The fog was all walls, and there was nothing to see in any direction. I tried to think.

'First, let me just get these paintings to the car,' I said, dropping to one knee and gathering the canvases. 'The mist will destroy them if we leave them lying out here. Who knows, I might be holding a minor masterpiece.'

Alison nodded. 'I'll go ahead and check the beach.'

'No. Come to the end of the path and wait for me. I'll be two minutes. Less than that, even. I don't want you going down there on your own. I don't want us getting separated, not in this weather. And the ground is bad, pitted with hollows that you won't see because of the grass. It'd be the easiest thing in the world to turn an ankle out here. And you definitely don't want to be alone if that happens. Wait on the path and then we'll go together.'

We walked back towards the slope then, she at my side

and occasionally touching my arm, my own hands occupied by the canvases pressed to my body. Visibility seemed
to be worsening and the whiteness now was almost absolute. At the bottom of the path we stopped, and she leaned
in awkwardly and kissed my mouth and then I hurried up
the incline towards the road, and the car, keeping to the
verge, conscious even then of worldly dangers. I opened
the car door and laid the canvases flat across the back seat.
Then, for a moment, I slumped against the side of the car. I
was trembling. The world had a locked-room stillness, but
I could hear the distant murmur of the ocean ebbing at
the shoreline, and the sense of hidden things lurking with
intent was very strong.

I hurried down the slope and stopped just where the
ground levelled out. Alison was not where I'd left her.

'Ali?'

The fog now felt barely penetrable. I strained to listen,
sure that she must be near, possibly within an arm's reach.
I turned and called out, lifting my voice a little and then
again a little more, not even attempting now to mask my
desperation, not caring. But I was alone. The fading day
played back nothing but its own beating heart, the soft,
low, relentless slop of the tide. Panic rose inside me, and I
roared Alison's name again and again, and the voice that

pushed up into the fog sounded only vaguely like mine, a hard rasping voice driven by terror and capable of seeing the worst even in its blindest state. Then, finally, away in the distance, I heard my own name, 'Michael', cracked in two, see-sawing in a childish, almost mocking way from syllable to syllable, and even through the smothering fog I was certain I recognised the voice as Alison's.

I had to resist the urge to charge blindly out into the day. The compass points had turned themselves around. I took several deep breaths and dropped down onto my haunches, the only thing I could think of to do. My name rang out again, its sauntering swing the slow jab of a skipping rhyme, and I let it come at me and tried to get a sense of its direction. By the fourth call, I felt that I could place it, somewhere ahead and a few degrees to my right. I followed, slowly, deliberately not answering, cautious of my footing on the broken pathway. There were other sounds too, random stabbings that at times felt close enough to make me flinch or catch my breath, but I pushed them away because the greater voice kept on, familiar and then only half so, but drawing me forward, my name filling the distance like the unhurried flap of a boat's foghorn.

And then, just ahead, I glimpsed her. A shape, no more than that, a smudge of grey in the whiteness. I almost ran to her. She stood on the edge of the beach, facing the ocean and had let down her hair. As I watched, she began to peel off her clothes, piece by piece – the cardigan, the blouse, the knee-length skirt. My name continued to ring out, a drone now, vague, pitching one way and then the other, sharing the emphasis. In reply, I uttered her name, but my voice reached barely above a whisper and she must not have heard because she didn't turn, or stop calling. She stepped out of her underwear just as I came to within touching distance, and the mist must have lifted around her, at least a little, because I could make out all the details of her body, the milky skin, the smoothness of her bottom dappled with the moisture of the fog, the way the chill air raised a rash of goosebumps across the flesh of her thighs and hips.

'Alison,' I whispered, close enough now that she would have to hear, and started to reach out for her. But instead of turning she moved forward into the tide. Without giving myself time to think I plunged in behind her and, just as she was about to go under, grabbed her arm. She rolled and began to thrash, but I kept hold, and her body twisted in the water, pulling her shoulder back, half-capsizing itself to reveal her right breast and the small puce stone of its rising nipple, and then her hair dropped away from her face and I saw that she was no longer Alison but a young woman, a girl of mid to late teens and almost beautiful. And as I watched, transfixed, her skin began to turn grey and then muddy, and her eyes, staring up at me, sank from a soft sky colour to the slime green of river weed. One temple had been crushed in with something blunt or smashed against rock, and the wound lay open as a treacle blackness hiding pearly yellow secrets deep inside. Stretched out on the water below me, she held my gaze and began to smile and then soundlessly laugh, and water wept from her nostrils and the corners of her mouth in a mixture of the fresh and putrid. And even as my hand loosened its grip, hers, cold and hard as wet stone, found my wrist and clutched me tight enough to hurt. I understood what she meant to do only an instant before it happened, and then she slipped beneath the surface. Manacled, I went under, too.

The coldness numbed me. I opened my eyes to murk, and for a moment, until I tried to breathe, it was not so different from being on land again, caught in that fog. This was heavier, and devoid of light, but the sensations of enclosure and blind confusion were the same. I flailed, causing a little air to escape my lungs, and then, through the flush of bubbles, I began to see blanched faces crowding in from all around. Childlike, the tendrils of their long hair rippling in a slow dance, their eyes wide and dead but somehow seeing, somehow knowing me. I screamed and felt it loud through my chest and throat, but outside of myself there was only the total press of the water, full of whispers. I burned to breathe but it was ocean that flooded in and held me while I kicked and tossed, thrashed to get away, to be above and once more taking in air. I clenched my eyes shut and felt my mind let go and madness start to take hold, but when I returned to the world again I was on my back on the sand, staring up into whiteness. Gradually, sounds closed in, the jerk and laboured breath of crying, not mine but Alison's, and when I reached out she took my hand and brought herself close for me to see. I let her kiss me and help me up, and we stood together, our clothes wet through, shivering so hard that we could feel the jarring of one another's bones.

'What happened to you, Mike? Why were you in the water?'

'I told you to wait,' I gasped.

She pulled her hair back from her face, and I saw her cheek smudged with grit or sand and attempted with my thumb to wipe it clean until I realised that it was not dirt at all but a graze.

'I meant to,' she said. 'Though I wasn't exactly happy at being on my own, even for those few minutes. But someone passed me in the mist. A shape, a shadow. I don't know. Very close, but without detail. I was certain that it had to be Maggie. Now I'm not sure what I saw. I tried calling out, but she was there and then gone, except for the sound of footsteps brushing through the long grass. So, I followed. What else could I do? And when I got to the beach, a breeze lifted the fog a little, and I saw her. The girl, not Maggie but just like the one you had described seeing. Standing on the rocks, naked, just like you'd said, with her hair down, facing the ocean.'

'Come on,' I said. 'Let's go back.'

'Where?'

'The car. Cork. Dublin. Anywhere, as long as it gets us away from here. Christ, I'm freezing.'

'But what about Maggie?'

'Maggie's gone. Even if she's all right, she won't come back here. The house is destroyed. We'll ask in the village. Maybe they got her out. Hopefully they'll at least know something.'

'Why were you in the water, Mike? What did you see?'

'Didn't you hear me calling you?'

'I thought I did. But the fog was so dense. Mike. Please. Tell me. What did you see?'

'Forget it,' I said. 'Let's just go.'

She took my arm, and we helped one another back up along the path. Evening had come in, the advancing hour causing the light to shift, a thickening of the whiteness that somehow made the fog more pliable. The stench of burnt timber continued to pollute each struggled breath, but we bore the taste and pressed on, keeping strictly to the path and careful of our footing. When the cottage seeped once more into view as a greyness ahead and to our right, we leaned away from it, skirting it in the widest possible sweep. Yet even then the sense of its menace felt absolute. As we passed, Alison tried to get one last look at the place, but I stepped in and prevented her, blocking the view with my body. Because she'd already seen too much. We both had. And because I was afraid. The windows had blown out with the heat of the fire and left dark gaping holes either side of the empty doorway. I kept my gaze averted, certain of what I'd see if I risked casting so much as a glance. Maggie in one window, silent and damaged, bedraggled, smeared with ash, watching us. And in the other, the taller figure of a man, the Master, the one I already knew. I didn't look because I didn't need to. Madness lay in that direction, and I'd already had a taste. I knew they were there and that they always would be, just as they'd always in some way be with me. Watching, smiling. Waiting. I tightened my

grip on Alison's arm and quickened our pace, desperate
for escape.

★

The darkening fog gave Allihies an otherworldly feel. The
day was not yet gone but the windows of shops and houses
were already lit and the few street lamps burned, triggered
by an obvious need, their fiery orange glow holding like
torches above the sloping street. There was nothing to see
of the mountains, fields and ocean, no hint of them, even,
except in how they held to within the fabric of the place.

Because it was still early, the pub was quiet. A young
blonde couple sat at a small round table beside the dead
fireplace – German, if the sound of their occasional mut-
terings was in any way truthful, the young man with a
lantern-jawed smirk huddling close while the girl, clearly
at ease with being in charge, shuffled her way through a
small bundle of photographs. At the end of the counter,
on a high stool, an old man in an overcoat and a flat cap
perched with arms folded and eyes closed, asleep or else
just taking the time to contemplate his half-finished pint
of stout and the accompanying drop of something hot. We
came in from the doorway and stood in the middle of
the lounge, but no one paid us any attention until a third

man, a stocky, middle-aged sort, wandered through from a storeroom, carrying a large red plastic crate of bottles. He pushed past, slipped behind the bar and set down the crate, then finally turned to us.

'What'll it be?' he said, his voice heavy with vibration, the sort of voice that probably broke repeatedly over the years but which had come to fit him well. He looked us up and down then, taking his time with Alison. 'Is it raining again? Christ, there's just no let-up with this weather.'

'Can you tell us anything about last night's fire?' I asked, and the old man to our left opened his eyes, and I knew that if I were to turn around I'd find the German couple watching, too.

'What fire is that?'

'A couple of miles out the road,' Alison said. 'A cottage. It's—'

'I know the cottage. But I know nothing about any fire.'

'Our friend lives there. Maggie Turner. She's an artist. Maybe you've met her. She moved in at the beginning of the summer, had the place completely renovated. But we've just been out there and it's destroyed. The stones are still hot, you can smell the ash on our clothes. We're worried. We tried searching for her, but the fog is so thick. We're hoping somebody around here might know something.'

The Dead House

The barman looked from one of us to the other.

'There was no wind last night. This mist has been in since late yesterday. Thick as well water, too. That'd have kept the smoke down. But I know the girl you're talking about. That is to say, I've seen her. We all have. Not often, mind, and not recently, but for the first couple of months or so after she moved here, she'd often call in for a cup of coffee. I suppose whenever she had shopping to do, or letters to post. Sometimes she'd ask to use the phone. Nice girl. That was my impression anyway. Kept mostly to herself, if I have her right, but friendly enough. The smiling kind. Maggie, you said her name was? That sounds about right. Rings a bell, anyway. She was English. I remember that. The accent. A timid little thing, but fair-looking.'

'Not that timid, I'd say.' The old man at the counter muttered the words at his glass. 'Not if she could bring herself to live in that house.'

I moved towards him. 'What do you mean?'

He looked up at me and then away, but not before I'd caught the white glint of the collar at his throat. A priest. Hard to put an age to, but a worn sort, with darkish blotches reddening the flesh of his cheeks and a mouth that couldn't settle even in its silent state.

'Lonely down there. By the water. And cut off from

everything. Not a place for a young woman, I'd have thought. Not a place for anyone, you ask me. The Master's cottage. Everyone around here knows the stories, and there's plenty will swear the sweet Jesus down out of Heaven professing to the truth of them. But your friend is not the first to be taken in by the place. And probably won't be the last. That's what it can do.'

'Stories,' the barman grunted. He winked at the Germans, one of whom mumbled a wisp of laughter. 'Second best way I know of to pass a wet night. Not that I'm questioning the word of a man of the cloth, like.'

'Say what you like, Jimmeen.' The priest's eyes were fixed hard on his shot glass. 'But I've seen more than my fill over the years. They'd not catch me down there of a night. Not alone. Nor yourself either. Put me right if you want but I'd back good money on that. It's not all just stories.'

He still hadn't looked up, but seemed to be waiting for something. Maybe, in his mind, he was reciting a prayer. Then, slowly, he reached out, lifted the whiskey glass to his mouth and drained it. The barman stood, a cold grin stuck to his face, and when the glass returned empty to the counter he found a bottle and refilled it almost to the brim.

After that, the talk fell away. Alison and I drank whiskey

too, the glasses pushed on us, with no mention of water
and no talk of money. I limited myself to sips, knowing that
I had to drive. The alcohol itself had no significant effect
on me, but the heat that filled my mouth and throat helped
to at least steady my shivering. I tried to explain some of
what had happened, but my words came out broken and
made little sense beyond the obvious details, and no one
in the bar offered anything in the way of encouragement
or, after I had finished, met my eye. I know how I must
have sounded, but I also know what I saw in the old man's
face, and, though it was slightly better hidden, in the barman's, when I mentioned the girl on the rocks. Alison and
I stood side by side, sipping at our whiskey, our clothes wet
through from the ocean, the water dripping from us onto
the flagstone floor, and once our glasses were empty I put a
sodden note on the bar and we muttered goodbyes and left.
There was nothing more to be said, except to one another.
Outside, the darkness had properly taken hold, and the village was still and silent. We got into the car, turned up the
heater to its highest setting and for several minutes just
sat there. I felt like I was trying to wake from a dream
that had too tight a hold on me. Then, at last, I started the
engine and followed the coast road slowly north-eastwards,
back to Castletownbere. Alison remained in the car while I

checked in three different pubs until I found a pay phone that worked, and I put a call through to the authorities, gave my name and contact details, and reported both the fire and the missing person.

And that was all.

Back in Dublin, late into the night, we took turns under the hottest shower imaginable before falling exhausted into bed to sleep in one another's arms. I woke first, some seven hours on, to a frail wash of sun pouring in through the bedroom window. It was neither early nor late, and there'd been no dreams, at least none that I could remember. Alison continued to sleep, an arm and thigh spread across me beneath the duvet. I ran my fingertips down and back up along the gentle curves of her body, feeling the kernels and indentations of her spine, the cool slats of her ribcage, the smooth furled wings of her shoulder blades. Then I kissed her, gently, until she smiled from inside her dreams and kissed me back, and for the couple of hours that followed we let nothing come between us, no unwanted thoughts, nothing to bring down what we were so busily raising up. And when, a few days later, it came time to leave, I didn't want to go. Alison cried, and I felt like crying too. Something had changed for me in a permanent way.

Part III

The Dead House

That was nine years ago. A long time, in some respects. A lifetime, if we let Hannah, our daughter, be our measure. Weeks, months even, can go by now without me thinking about what happened. As I said at the beginning, life has been good to me, and I am happy. Hannah fills our days, such a beautiful child. Every time she sees me, a light comes into her face, and my heart melts. I know that it probably won't always be like this, that the way girls are at seven is not the way they will necessarily be at seventeen. But, for now, life is good. I don't miss the world of art at all, or city living. It seems that for years I existed with a great hole inside me, the sort of emptiness I only became aware of after it had been filled. For that, I owe Alison a great debt. Having what you need as well as what you want, and knowing that you have it, must be the definition of contentment.

There are still moments, though, when the world seems to stop turning for me, usually when that increasingly pressing need of the bathroom, or a glass of water, drags me from bed during the smallest hours of the night, or when I am out walking, trying hard to be obedient to my doctor's orders, taking a brisk morning stroll into the village and back. When I am alone. And it is then that the memories encroach, and with them, the questions. I no longer look for answers, having accepted that sometimes there are simply none to be found. And nine years is a long time.

Maggie's body was never recovered. The fire was investigated and foul play quickly ruled out. The signs of infestation made it likely that rats had chewed through cable either in the attic or the walls, and the thatch, especially thatch dried out from a long, good summer, would have been tinder to a flame. This was the most logical scenario, and the one to which all the evidence pointed. According to the experts, the heat would have been immense, the thick stone walls acting like a cauldron, though the temperatures involved would have come nowhere near approaching the sort of numbers necessary for melting bone. A cursory glance made it clear that Maggie had not been in the cottage at the time of the blaze, but five men trained specifically for this kind of work still spent the better part of a working day combing through the dust, obscenely diligent in their search, knowing exactly what to look for, and exactly what meant what. Making certain. What mattered, it seems, was proving it beyond doubt.

Towards the end of the first week following her disappearance, a cardigan was found, sodden, in the grass inside the circle of standing stones that she had mentioned, which initially raised everyone's hopes of a positive outcome. Tests were done in the hope of turning up a trace of ash, but the results proved inconclusive, and it was generally agreed that either the garment had been left behind on some earlier visit or else the elements had washed it clean.

I spoke with the Gardaí often, helping them to gain some sense of her state of mind, at least as I had perceived it to be. Half a dozen times over a period of perhaps a couple of weeks, sitting in the canteen with various paired combinations of the same four officers, three men and a woman, sipping bad tea and worse coffee from heavy white mugs lined with the shadows of uncountable refills. Informal and unprompted, with no leading questions or suggestions of anything untoward, no insinuations of guilt or attempts at apportioning blame, but official interviews, nonetheless, with details logged in notebooks, to be transcribed later into ledgers or maybe even onto a computer. I didn't care. I talked and wanted to talk. I told myself that these people were the law, that they'd know how to filter my ramblings for the few essential facts, and they'd know what to do with those facts, even if I didn't.

They listened, sitting across from and beside me at the table, the woman particularly attentive, a broad-cheeked type of about thirty, with her country edges showing and her nut-brown hair clipped into a mannish shape that actually benefited from the wearing of a cap. She or one of the men would nod encouragement while I relived my visits to Allihies, and I'd slow my voice when I noticed them trying to jot down some morsel of detail, instinctively wanting to help, but more often I preferred not to look at them when I talked because the least shift in their expression sent me trawling back over what I'd just said, wondering what important words I'd missed and was still missing. When I could lower my eyes, the words flowed more easily, until nobody could have doubted their aimless truth. The thoughts spilt from me, recounting in scatter-shot fashion the house-warming weekend and the fun we'd had until the séance. The good, the bad, the best. Descriptions of my return visit felt jarring against the ease and pleasure of that first trip, but I could feel my audience lean in, sensing that this might be where the clues would lie, and I traced the table's laminated grain with my fingertips and spoke of the condition into which the cottage had fallen, and the shock I'd felt, the terror, at finding Maggie on the beach in so distant and dishevelled a state. Unaware, except perhaps on some deep-seated level which could later be denied or at least ignored, that this would be the last time I'd see her. I recalled for them our conversations, without checking myself, sure that the words held something of worth, some hint that answered everything. All I kept back were the things that made no sense, the glimpses, the feeling of foreboding.

I appreciated the officers' expressions of sympathy, and the way they seemed to accept how deeply I was feeling her disappearance, but I could sense a level of detachment, too. I'd provided them with several photographs, some dating back over the previous five years or so as well as a few that Alison had taken during the house-warming weekend, and they passed them back and forth amongst themselves and finally selected one for media distribution, a snapshot that really managed to capture some essence of who Maggie was: a beautiful young woman just turning to the camera, still bright with laughter, her hair pulled back from her face, her expression alive to the unseen magic of the world. They had chosen well, yet it was clear to me that their gazes were limited to surfaces, that they weren't trying, or were actively trying not to get to the heart of the picture, to really learn about the person smiling back at them from the glossy paper. Even as this registered with me, though, I understood their reasons.

Missing-person cases have become such a sad but inevitable fact of life in recent years, with something like a dozen new cases a day, countrywide. A ridiculous figure for a place like Ireland, with such a small population. Some don't want to be found. And too many turn up dead, either by their own hand or by another's. The first forty-eight hours tend to be critical. After that, the odds of a positive outcome hit exorbitant numbers. Handling such relentlessly grim statistics demands coldness. The sheer scale and quantity of the reports will crush all but the most hardened of hearts, and embracing cases on a personal level would be tantamount to suicide.

Our routine didn't vary a great deal. I talked, on something like half a dozen separate occasions, and they listened, sipping tea, watching me, and took what they felt might be worth taking, which unfortunately wasn't much. They circulated Maggie's identity, advised garda stations across the county as to her likely state of mind, keeping to within a hundred-mile radius initially, but then, after the media had taken the story into the papers, expanding the search nationwide.

Rosemary, her sister, flew in from Vancouver, and she did what she could to help keep the story alive. She seemed able for the media in ways that Alison and I were not, and she spoke with journalists, gave radio interviews and even organised a shop-window poster campaign. But something in her face, a bemusement in no way connected to humour, suggested a refusal not only to accept what was happening but to believe a single word of it. During her quiet moments, in the lounge of the hotel bar with a second or third vodka within reach, she'd look at us, her gaze slipping between my face and Alison's, and considering Liz, too, if she happened to be with us, like somebody awaiting the punchline of an enormous practical joke. She knew Maggie better than anyone, of course, and yet in some ways she didn't know her younger sister at all, because Maggie was impossible to ever really know. She existed on another plane, always had; always half in a room and half somewhere else, always dreaming. You only ever got to share a piece of her, a fact which, Rosemary insisted, over and over, had to be understood, and taken into account. I recognised these words as expressions of desperation, some staunch adherence to logic that allowed her to remain focused, and strong, but I also knew, from personal experience, that such barriers offered only temporary protection. And, eventually, fatigue broke her down, and the tears began to fall, swelling to a deluge that could not be stanched.

There were a few initial sightings, and one in particular, towards the end of the second week, that the Gardaí decided was worthy of serious consideration, a call logged in response to some national radio discussion, claiming to have seen, within that very hour, a woman matching Maggie's description in Dublin's Phoenix Park. Early thirties, five-two or five-three, slightly built, long dark hair, severely dishevelled appearance, apparently disoriented. The call had proven genuine but, after a frantic two-hour search of the park, was deemed a case of mistaken identity.

And that was the closest we came to finding her.

★

Time passes. Days turned into weeks, and, eventually, the search was scaled back. The investigation continued to limp along for quite a while, and remained open, but the mounting stockpile of new cases meant that ours was necessarily given a low-priority status. This was upsetting to everyone concerned, but understandable. The world appreciates grief, but can only wait so long before getting back to its turning. You either climb aboard or you get left behind.

A few days into November, back in London, I glimpsed something that left me cold. London wasn't where I wanted to be, but I had commitments to honour and felt as if I had no choice. And once I'd touched down, work had swallowed me up, deals I'd left hanging, new work to be flaunted or sold. Everyone understood, but nobody truly understood.

On the cold white afternoon in question, a couple of days after Halloween, I was in Piccadilly, in the back of a taxi and on my way to a late lunch with a sometime client who'd flown in from Madrid just to speak with me and who was interested in buying at least one and possibly more of Maggie's final paintings.

Initially, I refused to even consider parting with them, but within a few hours of bringing them home I knew they couldn't remain in my apartment. Having them so near filled me with the most awful and inexplicable sense of dread. I'd hung a few in my living room, and immediately the apartment had darkened, as if something was being sucked out of the world. Also, they looked too right on my walls, as if they'd been painted with my living room in mind. I sat there for hours, trying not to look at them but helpless to their pull. And that night, I suffered the most vile nightmares. Upon waking, I could only recall flashes, but I remembered, on some sensual level, blood, screams and a lot of laughter. Alison was in the dream, and I'd either seen or caused some terrible thing done to her. Worse, I'd pleasured in it. The following morning, even before boiling water for tea, I took the pictures down, wrapped them in linen sheets and locked them away in a wardrobe.

We'd hit some traffic, typical for the time of day, somewhere between noon and one. I had a newspaper and was scanning the stories without really reading them, and when I glanced out of the window Maggie was standing there. Part of the crowd, but hard against its flow, like a stepping stone in a fast stream, and not smiling, not moving, simply watching me as I slipped past.

I panicked, and startled the driver so much with my shout to stop that he hit the brakes hard, hurtling me into the back of the passenger seat. I jumped out with the car still rolling, severely twisted my ankle and almost fell in front of a delivery van coming too fast in the other direction, but when I made it onto the footpath, she was nowhere to be found. The street was thick with people, but I worked my way back through them anyway, wincing with every step but searching faces, desperate to know.

Finally, the taxi driver came and found me. Part of it undoubtedly had to do with securing a fare, though I think he also felt genuine concern for my well-being. At least on some level. He was my age or a little older, a short, thick-set Caribbean named Albert, with deep-brown heavily-lidded eyes and a restless mouth boasting a golden lower left cuspid that seemed to skew the symmetry of his face whenever he spoke or sighed. His expression was one of

wide-eyed strain, a constant underlying wince roughly
equal parts curiosity and despair, as if he'd recently come
through a degree of suffering and had not yet been able
to let go of its sense-memory. Even if he himself had seen
nothing untoward, the way he stared at me suggested that
he knew I'd seen something.

He helped me back to the taxi, which he'd parked il-
legally and in a hurry, blocking part of the lane, and a string
of cars blew their horns at us as they crawled past, and I
saw angry faces mouthing silent obscenities from behind
the windscreens but could think of nothing to do except
shrug my shoulders at some and try to ignore the rest. I got
in and explained that I'd seen somebody I used to know,
but he sat in the driver's seat without the engine running,
his body twisted into a half turn, and waited for the rest. So
I told him. Some, not all. Enough. He wore a white shirt
with short sleeves, nowhere near sufficient for the chill of
November, and the skin of his face and extremely thick
arms was a rich, ripe chestnut brown. My words fell into a
hole. When he laid an arm across the back of his seat, a pale
tangle of scars revealed themselves along its underside, all
the way to his wrist.

'You're searching,' he said, finally. 'And you should stop.
Sometimes it is better not to look. Better not to see.'

He was correct, of course, but the wound was still raw.

And then, some five weeks later, I began to experience chest pains. At first, I tried to ignore them. Alison was coming to spend Christmas with me, and I wanted everything to be perfect. Looking back, I must have known there was a problem, but at the time it was just easier to dismiss it as a symptom of the recent stress. The truth is that we don't give a lot of thought to our own mortality, especially with true middle age still just an insinuation. We probably can't afford to, not if we hope to keep functioning on what passes for a normal level. We tend to deny ourselves glimpses of the end that awaits us all, at least until the big warnings come, the stab of pain running up your shoulder and neck, the moments of paralysis, the dull ache that fills your throat, that hollowed-out deadness similar to what you feel when you need to cry but can't. Still, we cope in the ways we know, and for me that meant long shifts at the office. Chipping away at my backlogged workload with twelve- and fifteen-hour days, trying to ensure that the time I'd have with Ali would be free of distraction. It was busy work, laden with phone calls, emails, invoices, visits to galleries, meetings with gallery owners, artists and buyers, but better that way, because I needed the activity of the chase.

Because my problems limited themselves, initially, to twinges, they seemed a natural reaction to the trauma of Maggie's disappearance and leaned towards a diagnosis of tension coupled with some kind of delayed shock. But over the next couple of days and nights the pain grew more extreme until, finally, I became frightened enough to seek medical help.

The doctor at the surgery was a very thin, very young-looking Indian man, dressed in a white lab coat worn open over mismatched grey-green slacks and tartan shirt, and he examined me in thorough fashion, then sat side-on to his desk and began to scrawl something on a plain white note-pad. He said, without looking up, that I was on the precipice of a heart attack. That was the word he used: precipice. The word alone almost knocked me off balance. If I'd waited another day, he said, it'd probably have been too late. But the critical thing now was to get my levels stabilised. My blood pressure was brimming against some danger-ous numbers. The note that he held out to me, folded in two, was not a prescription but a letter of admission to the hospital, and I was sent to sit in reception while calls were made and a bed found.

It happens that quickly. Life can change on the spin of a coin. Much of what followed for me had the quality of a dream. I remember the hospital bed, the whiteness and silence of the room with sleet falling against the glass. I remember waking after the bypass surgery to find Alison at my bedside, her face stretched and washed out from crying but trying hard to smile, holding onto my hand as if I were a kite that would drift away when released, that could be taken by the least breeze. I remember lying there in the night, with the hallway lit yellow beyond the ward's double doors, certain that there'd be no such thing as a new morning for me, certain with the occasional slap of every distant footstep that my time was drawing to a close. In those moments, I tried not to think about Maggie, but it seemed as if she was always there, on the edge of things, just out of sight but watching, and to be glimpsed if I was unlucky enough to turn my head quickly enough in the right, or wrong, direction.

★

My health problems heralded some necessary lifestyle adjustments. More than that, though, they focused my mind, and Alison's too, on what truly mattered to us. From that point on, our commitment deepened. By the time I was released from hospital, just before New Year's Eve, she had already made herself at home in the apartment. A couple of friends were looking after the gallery, she said, and she was here to look after me. I'd given her such a fright, she added, later, during one of the nights that followed. Lying beside me in the dark, probably afraid to move. She'd been sure she was going to lose me. Up until then, she'd handled me as if afraid I'd crumble beneath her touch. To be honest, I harboured similar thoughts. The least exertion seemed to threaten me. But that night I came to the realisation that I was not fragile. I'd been through something, yes, but I'd survived. And if I wasn't right yet, I soon would be. Time would correct the missteps. And I wasn't going to break. I cleared my throat, stared up into the blackness and asked if she'd marry me. At first, she didn't even answer, and for a few seconds I wondered if she might have fallen asleep, but then I felt the jerk of her breath and knew that she was crying. 'Okay,' she said, when she could.

So, we settled down. Alison sold the gallery, for a price that sounded good in cash terms but left her with only modest pocket money once she'd cleared the mortgage, and I scaled back on work, slipping into a sort of semi-retirement, and made arrangements towards a permanent and complete exit. I had savings, and a pension that lived up to about two-thirds of its promises, so we've been able to get by. Not to live as kings and queens, but who'd really want that?

Initially, home continued to be the apartment, which was still big enough for two and suitable for our needs, and then, a year and a half or so in, while touring the Cornish coast, we happened across Southwell, and the house we live in now, a place that seems to have been built with us in mind. Still within easy walking distance of civilisation, but rural enough, with its hulking skies, swathes of woodland and elevated sea views, to encourage the sense that the world was only us and what we could see, with nothing in between. And maybe the sea air added vigour because, by the end of year two, Ali fell pregnant, something that we'd each secretly hoped for but which neither of us had really expected, assuming, I think, without a word of discussion, that our time had passed us by.

Details fade with the years. We don't necessarily forget the big moments, but they lose the edge of their flavour. Life, just living, is so much more interesting. Yet even so, there are still nights, even now, when I'll be lying awake while Ali sleeps, or sitting at the kitchen table so that I can read a book and drink tea without disturbing her, and I'll think again about how easily I could have died, how convoluted it must have been for the stars to align themselves in my favour. If I'd stayed in bed that day instead of visiting the doctor, if I'd kept to the insistence that the pain was just exhaustion, nothing a couple of sleeping pills wouldn't cure, I really do believe that I'd probably have slipped away. In my apartment, alone. Knowing that my heart could have burst without anyone to hold my hand or answer my strangled gasps for help is the stuff of which hauntings are made and a big part of the reason why I take so little risk with sleep even now, these nine years on. That's the lottery. But I made it through.

Alison and I are easy in one another's company. Always have been, I think. We have our down days, like every couple, but they no longer define us. Contentment, as I've said before, is the word that probably best describes the life we found together, and that state has only deepened since Hannah was born. We are a family, and we live for one another. Which is as it should be. And given how fortunate I've been, I suppose it is to my shame that, over time, my thoughts have turned less and less towards Maggie. I've never forgotten her, of course; as well as being responsible for Alison and me finding one another, she was too important to me, and too dear a friend, to ever completely vanish from my life. The memories are never too far from reach, and if they sometimes manage to stir awake a smile then they are also invariably infused with sadness and tend to drain the light from even the most brilliant of days. But it's been years since I've spoken of her with anyone, even Ali. In general, it's fair to say that her colours have dimmed, and she simply no longer fits within my daily conversations. Perhaps if I was the praying kind she'd have remained closer to my surface, but maybe it's for the best that I'm not and that she hasn't. Because, these days, my duties lie in other directions.

★

Our home, as I've already explained, sits on an acre or so of slightly sloping wood-backed land. The natural fall of the ground gives the rear of the house an elevated perspective, and from the small kitchen/conservatory doorway we are afforded stunning views of an ocean unbroken except for the tan-grey scatter-shot of some interrupting islets, an ocean that breathes and bleeds with the day and boasts a thousand different skins. Away to the east, the land bends back on itself and folds down into the harbour before rising up again beyond in a long yellow-white run of cliffs. We have a good stretch of back garden, mainly lawn but with a reasonably sized vegetable patch, off to one side, that yields the mainly summer crops of lettuce, onions and cabbage, with a couple of twenty-foot runs of potatoes coming in a little later in the year.

I keep the grass mown, largely out of habit and, I suppose, a predilection for order that probably says quite a bit about me as a man, and then, some forty or fifty strides out, the woods begin, a dense copse of alder, beech and dwarf oak that helps shield us from the worst of the ocean winds. Some generation of previous owners had furrowed a pathway through the trees so as to link up with the walking trail that follows a long stretch of the coastline, and, while their intentions were, I'm sure, entirely practical, the path has over time taken on a distinctly romantic aspect, its narrow, winding nature, and the soft uttering of the breeze among the branches, practically insisting on hand-in-hand walks of those in love. People often speak of it in the village, having long since accepted it as part of the local lore, and I can understand why. At the high end of a lazy summer's evening, with the late red light coming in flecks through the canopy, a loved one at your side and the nightingale in fullest song, I can imagine nowhere like it in the world.

Beyond these trees, the walking trail veers to within a few yards of the cliff edge, but heavy snatches of briar act as a natural protection, and it is safe enough for Hannah to play there, even with a minimum of supervision. She loves the woods, loves climbing and building camps and trying to identify the birds that come, by their calls as well as their plumage, loves watching the leaves change shades in the autumn and collecting them when they fall so that she can bring them into school. She's edging into that age bracket now, beyond the baby stage and before the cocky cynicism of the late pre-teens, when the colours of the world for her have found their fire. Nature captivates her: spiders and their webs, the milky coin-sized crabs that scuttle in and out of the rock pools down along the shore, the fusion of small noise that is always there and will reveal itself and unravel if you let yourself be still and silent long enough to hear.

She can spend entire weekends outside, playing her games, exploring, imagining, dreaming, and even when the weather turns rainy, her play, safe beneath the shielding trees, doesn't tend to suffer much in the way of interruption. In fact, rain brings something new to the equation, new smells, new sounds.

But today, at lunchtime, after two very still and dry late April weeks, the rain came in a deluge, driving her inside. Another Sunday. Christ, the fools that time can make of us. When I remember how the Sundays of my own childhood could stretch to nearly never-ending length, I am stunned at how years can be so fleeting and how they can lay themselves in layers one upon the next so that no point of the past ever feels fully beyond reach.

Alison was in the kitchen, making sandwiches. Cheese and home-made pickle, always the majority choice in our household. I had the armchair beside the living-room window, idling through one of the newspaper's accompanying magazines. The back door must have been open, because the sound of Hannah's running steps made me turn my head. Girls of six or seven usually run, if walking can be at all avoided, and the rain alone should have been reason enough, if one were needed. But I knew, even before I saw her glance behind her, that there was something more than rain involved.

Out of instinct, I turned my attention to the woods, thinking, I suppose, that there could have been someone there, a stranger. Southwell is safe, but nowhere is completely safe, not any more. We all watch the news, we all know the monsters that exist.

The downpour blurred the world outside, greying everything, giving the woods in the near distance a warped, skeletal pallor. I wiped a hand across the striated glass, but, of course, nothing changed because nothing could.

Hannah came in and looked at me. Her eyes were big, uncertain. I could see her working out the permutations, and there was a moment when I was sure that she had something to say, but she kept silent, and after half a minute she turned away and dropped down onto the floor in a sitting position, legs to the side, in front of the television. The screen was lit with racing from Newmarket, the sound muted. She stayed with the gallop until its finish, and I watched her and waited.

'Dad?'

'Yes, sweetheart?'

'Are tricks always funny?'

She sat perfectly still, her tossed, straw-coloured hair hanging in flumes down her back and around her narrow shoulders. Her voice had a forced calm that quivered along its lowest edges.

'Not always,' I said. 'Some are funny, some clever, and some just mean.'

'That's what I thought.'

On the screen now, a woman, dressed for a winter that no longer existed and with a microphone attached to a longish pole, was interviewing someone I assumed to be the winning jockey, a surprisingly old-looking man in pink and green silks. He had a hawkish, mud-spattered face and appeared to take little outward pleasure at his victory.

'I think somebody is trying to play a trick on me,' Hannah said, and she turned and looked up at me over one shoulder. 'A mean one.'

'What happened?'

She thought about it. 'Nothing, really. I just heard something. A voice.'

'What kind of voice?'

She shrugged. 'I don't know. Just a voice. But like somebody lost. Maybe in a fog or something. A woman. And she was calling you.'

'Me?'

'Your name. Mike. That's what it sounded like. Over and over.'

'Are you sure?'

'I don't know.'

'There are lots of people named Mike. Maybe it was just somebody out on the trail, calling a child.'

'I told you. It was the woman.'

I went cold. 'What woman?' I asked, trying to keep my voice from caving in. 'Do you know her?'

'She comes to the path. Sometimes she's at the edge of the woods. I don't know her name. But I've seen her picture. In Mammy's drawer. The woman doesn't speak to me, but she sees me. I think she knows who I am. Sometimes, I'll be playing, and when I look up she'll be standing there. Watching. The others, too.'

My heart was beating so hard I could feel it in my throat. The air around me felt suddenly reduced. 'The others?' I whispered, when I could, and again I turned my gaze on the window, and the woods beyond. Aside from the rain, which was coming down hard, all was still.

'A girl, a bit older than me. With long black hair. And a tall man, dressed in black. They don't speak, and they stand back a little.' Ever so quietly, she cleared her throat. 'They scare me,' she added, in a murmur.

I ran outside. Within seconds I was drenched, and then the trees closed in around and above, shielding me. Caging me. My breathing came very loud, and the sound of the rain in the trees had a dense, rattlesnake insistence, but nothing moved. I looked around, then pushed my way through onto the path and followed it until the woods cleared and I met the trail, and the cliffs. As far as I could see in every direction, I was alone. Ahead of me, sea and sky had become one, a grey, swimming sameness that obliterated lines and seemed calm until its waves broke huge against the rocks somewhere out beyond the briar and down below.

Epilogue

Tonight, all we can do is sit up late, trying to make sense of things. Alison is crying. I've opened the bottle of nicely aged single malt that I'd been keeping for a night of celebration or need. I suppose this counts. Since becoming a father, I've largely sworn off hard liquor, but I make it a long way down the bottle's neck before even the most medicinal heat kicks in.

'Is this real?' Ali asks. We've lit a fire, which gives the room its only light, and she studies the flames with a trance-like devotion. Shadows seem to shift the skin of her yellowed face, and her wide eyes shine. I can see what the tears have done.

'I think so,' I say. 'How can it not be?'

'Could she have overheard something, though? Even by accident?'

'I don't see how. We haven't spoken of this in years.'

'Coincidence, then. A family out walking. Maybe we're overreacting, filling in blanks that don't exist.'

I shrug, and empty my glass in a swallow. Then I count in my mind before reaching again for the bottle. Giving up at twenty-five, I pour.

'What do you suppose it means, Mike?'

'I think they want something. And there's no getting away from them.'

'Oh, Jesus.'

'Yeah.'

'The voice she heard. Your name.'

'I know. But it's not me that they've been watching.'

There is something about the silence that descends on us then. I sit still until I can no longer bear to do so, and then I get up and wander through the house. All the lights are out, but I think I fear the brightness more than the dark. Because at least in the dark I will not have to see what might be waiting. I climb the stairs, slowly, trying not to make the steps creak. Hannah's bedroom door is shut, and I lean against it for several seconds, weighing the silence beyond, then ease the handle down and push it open, just a few inches. A night light is burning, with a shade that sprays onto the ceiling the shapes of stars and crescent moons, and she is asleep, sprawled on her side at a short diagonal across the bed, having wrestled loose of the duvet, her pyjama-clad legs scissoring towards the mattress's low corners. The curtains are drawn, blocking off the view of the woods and water, and I feel grateful for that. I ease myself into the room, spread the duvet over her again and lean in to set a kiss on her forehead. She stirs against my lips, wrinkling her nose, but doesn't wake.

Downstairs, Alison has filled my glass nearly to its brim

and is drinking from it. I don't explain where I've been, and she doesn't need to ask.

'I'm cold,' she says, and she moves down onto the floor and draws herself in closer to the fire. I stand for a moment longer, then sit down in my armchair. The only sounds then are the low crackle of the fire and a clock dryly ticking. The silence comes again, crushing, and I let it, knowing that it's useless to fight. And when I am overcome with the need to hide away, I reach for the bottle and hold on. In the distance, something or someone screams or cries out. I am used to the sound of gulls, and I tell myself that's what I'm hearing. Alison, not ready for doubt, does not look up.

★

The unexamined life is not worth living. I've spent years burying what happened in Allihies, but those memories are like the body in the bog. Time has stood still for them, their details remain fine as coal dust, ready after all that darkness to shine, and burn. The past will not remain the past.

By recounting my story, I suppose my hope was that I might uncover some kind of explanation. But beneath the bandage there is only the wound. Our foolishness opened a door back then, exposing something of insatiable appetite.

Something monstrous.

After nine years, I'd almost forgotten, assuming, I suppose, that, having paid our price, we'd left it all behind us. But escape is never total, and we'd been wrong, Alison and I, to stop running. And now, again, it seems they've found us.

Hannah said she heard my name being called, and I believe her, but I think she misunderstood. I think what she heard was actually a warning to me, not a call. And that frightens me more than anything else. Because something is here, and running now is not an option. I've already lost a lot, but there's always more to lose.

That's why I am afraid.